NOT WITHOUT ANNA

NOT WITHOUT ANNA

VICKI M. TAYLOR

Mundania Press

NOT WITHOUT ANNA
Copyright © 2004 by Vicki M. Taylor

A Mundania Press Production

Mundania Press LLC
6470A Glenway Avenue, #109
Cincinnati, Ohio 45211-5222

To order additional copies of this book, contact:
books@mundania.com
www.mundania.com

Cover Art © 2003 by Ariana Overton
Titling and Layout by Stacey L. King
Composition and Design by Daniel J. Reitz, Sr.
Production And Promotion by Bob Sanders
Edited by Daniel J. Reitz, Sr. and Audra A. F. Brooks

ISBN: 1-59426-051-6

First Trade Paperback Edition • January 2004
Library Of Congress Catalog Card Number: 2003114038

Printed In The United States of America

10 9 8 7 6 5 4 3 2 1

Dedication

To my daughter, Michelle.

Prologue

"Come on, Anna. Hurry up!" Mike called from the car parked in the driveway.

"Wait a sec," pleaded Anna from the doorway of the house. "I gotta say bye to my mom." She disappeared back in the house with a slam of the door.

The rest of the teenagers slumped dejectedly in their seats. Jeff, the driver of the car, turned accusing eyes toward Mike. "Look, man," he began his typical tirade. "You said she'd be ready. Let's just go."

"No," Mike yelled. "Not without Anna."

"Jeez, don't you two ever do anything apart?" The question came from the backseat. Jessie, the youngest of the group and still a junior in high school didn't quite understand Mike and Anna's explosive relationship; they were either fighting or making out. Her hair was cut short, like a pixie, and dyed a deep magenta with bright yellow tips. Her outward appearance matched her personality. She was open and outgoing.

"Yeah," said Mandy insolently. "You're like freaks." She nervously touched the delicate gold filigree hoop protruding from her left nostril. She had it pierced a week ago, but it was still tender. She resented Anna's intrusion on their group and she resented Mike dumping her last year for Anna.

"Shut up, Mandy." Mike said with no malice in his voice. From experience, he knew the best way to handle Mandy when she got in one of her moods was to not provoke her and eventually she'd get over it.

But Mandy wasn't in the mood to just let it go. "You sure spend a lot more time with her than you ever did with me."

Mike slammed his hand down hard on the plastic and vinyl console between the two bucket-style front seats. "Look, guys. Anna is my girlfriend," he pointedly stared at Jeff who was drumming impatiently on the steering wheel. "If she doesn't go, I don't go."

Jeff threw up both hands in surrender. "Ok, fine. Damn, boy. Take a pill or something." He looked up at the sound of the front door slamming. "Be cool, man. Here she comes."

With a quick kiss, Mike helped Anna into the car and they sped away from the quiet suburb of Anna's neighborhood to spend another hot, muggy weekend night cruising the streets of their hometown with other bored teenagers. Looking for something, anything that could keep them entertained until they got bored and moved on, always searching for the next thrill.

Chapter One

Splash.

Floating lazily in the pool, Jessie wiped the heavily chlorinated water from her eyes that splashed up over her face.

Splash.

Not funny.

Irritated, Jessie rolled over onto her stomach to see who was making waves. She scanned the surface of the pool looking for a smirking face.

Boys are so immature. They think it's so cute to be annoying.

She searched for the source of the waves. Of all the teenagers in the pool, no one looked guilty enough to have been purposely splashing water at her.

It figures.

Then she saw them.

What are they doing?

Shadowed in the corner of the deep end, near the eight-foot marker—Anna and Mike.

Oh ... Mike.

Jessie watched Mike cup his hand under Anna's chin. For a brief second, jealousy openly flickered across her face.

Mike, you should be my boyfriend.

Day and night, she daydreamed about him. Tall, cute, tan. Popular. Did he even know she was alive? Hardly. Instead, the object of her crush preferred the Barbie doll-type.

Anna.

For the life of her, Jessie couldn't figure out why. They argued all the time, but seemed obsessed with each other. Inseparable. Totally. Just like they were right now.

Unable to stop her morbid curiosity, Jessie stayed where she was and watched the pair as they moved about in the water oblivious to their audience.

Mike's back faced toward her while his body blocked most of her view. Jessie could see Anna's arms wrapped around Mike's neck and her fingers clutching his dark, wet-slicked hair. A glint of silver flashed in the bright moonlight.

I helped him pick out that bracelet for her.

Slightly embarrassed, Jessie half-stared, even while trying to look away. Engrossed, she watched Mike move his body against Anna's, causing the water to ripple out as small waves. Anna's legs kicked out, side to side. Water splashed the sides of the pool.

Jessie's mouth gaped open.

Oh, God! Are they doing it? Right in the pool?

Embarrassed to be caught staring, she abruptly turned her head. In doing so, the flash of silver again captured her attention. Without self-control, she held her breath and stared.

It looks like it hurts.

Anna's fingers gripped Mike's hair so tight it looked like she would tear it out by the roots. In a few seconds, the fingers relaxed, then slid to Mike's shoulders.

Was that it?

Exhaling abruptly, Jessie couldn't bear to look at them any longer. With powerful strokes, she pushed herself through the water toward the opposite side of the pool, hoping it looked like she hadn't seen anything.

Shuddering, she reached out and grabbed the side of the pool intent on getting out. She couldn't get the image of Mike and Anna out of her mind.

In the pool. How gross could they be?

She pulled herself up out of the water and sat on the side of the pool, letting her legs dangle over the edge. With both hands, she pushed her short, spiky hair back from her forehead.

Were they really doing it?

Water drops ran in tiny rivulets down the side of her face. Swiping her hands down her arms, then down her thighs, she sluiced most of the water from her petite, boyish body. The one-piece tank suit she wore fit snugly, without bunching at her waist. Another swipe of her hands and she easily compressed most of the water out of her suit.

Big boobs. That's what the guys liked.

With familiar regret, she sighed silently as her hands slid over the nearly unnoticeable bumps that passed for breasts on her small chest. What was it her mother had called her? A "late bloomer."

Jessie pictured her mother's tiny frame and barely distinguishable breasts. Somehow, she didn't think that all the patience in the world was going to change genetics. With any luck, she might have inherited a little bit of her father's genes. At six foot, he towered over her mom.

She sighed again, this time blowing it out in a loud whoosh. Kicking her feet in the water, she only hoped she didn't inherit his dorky-looking legs.

"Hey, Jess."

Jessie craned her neck up to see who was standing next to her. "Hey, John, what's up?"

"Here, have a drink of this."

"What is it?" Jessie asked as John handed her a plastic cup half filled with fizzing red liquid.

John smiled his slow little smile. "Just a little of this and a little of that."

Jessie grinned back. "John, come on," she said half-seriously. "You know I don't drink anything when I don't know what it is."

"Alright," John laughed, "you little wussy, it's just some Hawaiian Punch and 7-up. Feel better?"

"No booze?"

"Nah, it's all we had left in the apartment. Go ahead, drink it." John squatted down next to her and tousled her short, magenta-dyed hair. Even though it was dark, he could still see the bright yellow tips reflecting in the light. "Besides, I think it's time we all started sobering up, anyway. Cool?"

"Cool."

Jessie smiled at John and leaned over to lay her head on his arm and sipped her drink. John Cooper had been her best friend for as long as she could remember. Even though he was two years older than her and just graduated from high school, they still hung out together.

Too bad I can't feel about John like I feel about Mike.

Jessie tilted her head back. "Your mom is going to be so pissed when she gets home and finds all her booze gone."

She watched his eyes narrow and darken, and then he turned his head away and said, "Yeah, well, maybe she'll be too drunk to notice."

Jessie could feel John's muscles tense up where his shoulder touched hers. He got that way every time his mom went on one of her binges. She put the empty glass next to her on the pool deck. It fell over and rolled a short distance. Instead of reaching over to pick it up, she decided to lighten the mood.

Jabbing an elbow to John's ribs, she prodded, "hey, you only graduate from high school once, ya know." Another jab. "Although, in your case I'm sure they could make an exception."

The next jab went into empty space and she nearly fell over with the force. With no time to react, Jessie found herself sliding over the edge of the pool and the next second she was over her head into the water.

As she sputtered to the surface, she saw John standing on the edge of the pool. His laughter rang in her ears. Her mouth full of water, she spit as hard as she could and hit him full in the chest. Instantly, he picked up a pool chair as if to throw it at her.

Pretending fear, her shriek of laughter resounded in the night air. It drew a combination of shushes and questions from the rest of the teenagers scattered about the pool area.

John put his fingers to his lips and whispered loudly. "Shhhhhhhh ... you wanna wake up the whole apartment complex?"

Jessie blew him a kiss and turned over on her back to float in the water.

He really is my best friend. Well, my best friend, next to Anna.

Smiling, she half-closed her eyes and laid her head back further into the water. Her ears filled and suddenly she was surrounded by a rushing noise. It was loud, after the stillness above the water. She closed her eyes completely and listened to the water rushing around her ears as she paddled her hands gently to keep herself from sinking.

The water was warm, almost tepid, like cooling bath water. The day had been hot, nearly ninety-seven degrees, a new record, or so the weatherman had boasted. With the humidity, it felt more like a hundred and ninety-seven.

Well, okay, so it wasn't quite that hot. But, it could have been. What were a few degrees here or there? Especially when they'd broken another record today.

Why did weathermen get so excited about new high temperature records, anyway? Were weathermen in hell as excited about rising temperatures? Did they get ecstatic over new records too?

Dipping one hand in the water, Jessie splashed the water on her face to cool down. Still high from the joint she'd smoked earlier and all the beer she drank, she giggled at the image of a weatherman giving a forecast for hell.

"Hello, folks, looks like another scorcher today. We'll beat our old record of nine hundred and forty-three degrees."

She giggled again, just because. The night air pressed down, forcing her giggle back to her like it bounced off an invisible barrier. What a really weird night.

She lifted her head to look around. Through glazed, red-rimmed eyes, from too much chlorine and too many drugs, what Jessie saw made her giggle again. This time, a nervous giggle. Like she saw something funny, but it wasn't really funny.

How weird. Like some bizarre scene out of a horror movie.

Most of the other teenagers were still in the water, all floating, either on their backs or fronts. No one was making a lot of noise. The obscure muted image of the full moon reflected eerily in the nearly still water of the swimming pool.

Intermittently, the image would shimmer and be broken by a lazy slap of a hand or kick of a leg. The effort would be just enough to keep someone floating on top of the water away from the wall so they wouldn't bump their head.

An anxious shiver coursed through Jessie's body. She wondered if Stephen King ever had an image like this in his mind while writing his books. Teenage bodies floating in a pool in the middle of the night.

She shivered again at the creepiness of her thoughts.

Next thing I'll start imagining monsters attacking.

Taking a deep breath, she breathed in the wild jasmine. Night air in Florida always smelled so good.

Summer was just starting and Jessie was with the coolest group of kids in town. All her hard work had paid off. This was going to be the best summer ever. Next year she'd be a senior and hanging out with the best crowd.

Life was good.

Making a vow to herself, Jessie promised that no matter what it took, she'd be the number one girl of the group this time next year. Who else would take the place of the most popular girl, but the most popular girl's best friend?

Not like I didn't earn it, this year.

Covering for Miss Goody-Two-Shoes for the last few months should get her in if nothing else did. Jessie experienced a small twinge of guilt and looked up quickly to see if the target of her thoughts was anywhere nearby. She liked Anna—a lot—and most times they got along really well, usually telling each other everything. But, sometimes Jessie felt so inferior to her friend.

It's so unfair.

Some people got everything—looks, brains, boys, luck—while others, like her, had to make do with leftovers.

Jessie's eyes skimmed the water and found the familiar cloud of blond hair. Anna was in the corner of the deep end—without Mike for once. She lay still, floating on the water. *She even made floating in the water look beautiful.*

Hastily dismissing Anna from her thoughts, Jessie turned to look for Mike. Maybe she could go talk to him for a few seconds without Anna interrupting.

Deep in the back of her mind she knew it was useless to think she would ever be anything but just a kid to him. Just the kid who hung out with him and Anna.

Well, all that was going to change this year.

Jessie was at Anna's house when she got her college acceptance letter today. She was waiting for Anna to tell Mike. As far as she knew, Anna hadn't told him yet. She was sure she'd know when Anna did because Mike was bound to hit the roof.

Jessie recalled their talk earlier that day when they were finalizing plans—and collaborating stories—for tonight. Anna said that Mike was going to be so pissed when he found out she was accepted to the college in California. The strange thing was, Anna said she didn't care what Mike thought.

Jessie remembered how surprised she was to see the determined look of defiance in Anna's eyes. Not wanting to get caught up in another one of Anna's tirades about how much Mike loved her and didn't want to be away from her, Jessie had quickly changed the subject.

Now, Jessie wondered if Anna had told Mike at all. Maybe he didn't take it as hard as Anna thought he would. Jessie imagined that Anna exaggerated quite a bit when it came to Mike's devotion to her. She sometimes thought that Anna wouldn't be as easy to get along with if she didn't have as much attention as she did. Anna was a pretty high maintenance friend.

Jessie made her way over to where Mike was sitting and plopped down next to him on the lounge chair.

"Hi, Mike," she sing-songed and was immediately rewarded with a gagging reflex motion from John who stood close enough to hear her. "Whatcha doin'?"

"Hi, Jessie," Mike automatically responded as he nervously looked over his shoulder toward the pool.

Jessie followed his gaze. Anna. Of course. But this time, Anna didn't rush over immediately and throw herself in between Mike and anyone else.

She hasn't seen us yet. Good.

Jessie figured she probably had a few minutes before Anna decided Mike had been on his own long enough and she needed to be the center of his attention.

"Creepy, huh?"

"What?"

Jessie nodded her head toward the pool where most of the group was still in the water. "All the floating bodies. Like a scary movie."

"Yeah, pretty creepy, I guess."

Jessie jumped when Mike reached out and stroked her hair.

"Pretty color."

"Uh, thanks." Jessie fingered a short lock.

Mike's touching me.

"I colored it special, for the graduation."

Stupid thing to say.

Jessie tried again. "Anna helped me, did she tell ya?"

Without responding, Mike stared off into the distance with a strange look on his face.

Jessie waited for him to answer, and when he didn't she rubbed her sweaty palms on her knees and tried a new topic. "So, Mike, have you heard back from any of the colleges you applied at?"

"Huh?" Mike jumped as if he had been pinched. "What makes you ask that?"

"Just wondering if you were going to be around next year," Jessie replied. "Hey, are you okay?"

"Sure, why?"

"I dunno, you just seem distracted, is all."

"I've got a lot on my mind, Jessie." Mike said with an impatient gesture. "Decisions, you know, stuff like that."

Smiling brightly, Jessie patted his arm gently and said, "Okay, okay. Take it easy. Jeez."

"Hey, there's Paul, he's supposed to have my smokes. Later."

Abruptly, Mike stood and walked over to where Paul was intently embroiled in a discussion with two other guys. Jessie stared at his retreating backside as the smile faded slowly from her face.

"Give it up, Jess." John said as he sat down in the space Mike vacated and gave Jessie a brotherly hug.

Jessie pushed John's arm away. "Give what up? I was just trying to talk to the guy."

John raised his hands in a sign of apology. "Okay. My mistake." He glanced at his watch and sighed. "Three o'clock. God, no wonder I'm tired."

Jessie swallowed her pride and pushed her disappointment about Mike out of her mind. She grinned back at her friend. Playfully punching him in the arm she said, "Awww, poor baby, you already getting so old you can't party like you used to?"

"I'll never get too old to beat the crap out of you, you little runt."

Jessie squealed as John tickled her unmercifully until in mutual surrender they stopped to rest.

Panting from their physical exertion, John's face became serious. "Look, Jess. He's not worth it."

Jessie rolled her eyes. "I know, I know, he's not good enough for me, right?"

"Right. That's the attitude." John stood and clapped his hands, then rubbed them together briskly. "Okay, then. Glad that's settled. Now, how about helping me kick everybody outa here before we get busted?"

John yelled out to the group that it was time to pack it in and head home.

Jessie stood and impulsively hugged her friend. "Thanks."

John hugged her back, holding her close. "Hey, I don't suppose your mom knows that you're here, does she? You got a place to stay?"

"Yeah, I told her I was staying the night at Anna's."

"You guys are gonna get in trouble one of these days." John said as he started gathering plastic cups and putting them in a large black plastic trash bag.

"Nah, we got it covered. We do this all the time."

"Don't come running to me if you get grounded for the rest of your life." John flashed a sudden grin. "Again."

Playfully, Jessie pushed John away. "Shut up."

John shoved back. "No, you shut up."

"No, you shut up."

"Whiner."

Jessie scrunched up her face and stuck out her tongue. "Dork."

John opened his mouth to retort, but was interrupted by a tall, perfectly proportioned redhead pulling on his arm.

"John, can you make them get out of the pool? They're not listening to me." Amanda pouted and clung to John's arm with a hand of brilliantly painted, ridiculously long, purple nails.

Jessie mumbled under her breath. "Jeez, talk about a whiner."

"I heard that," Amanda said. She looked contemptuously down her nose at Jessie and waved her brightly colored hand in a dismissive gesture while she ran her other hand down her curved hip in a practiced pose. "Go bother somebody else, little boy."

I'll show you a little boy, you big fat cow.

Seething, Jessie balled her hands into fists, ready to knock Amanda on her perfectly shaped ass. Before she could even take the first swing, John pulled Amanda aside, handed her the trash bag, and asked her to finish picking up the plastic cups while he took care of the slackers in the pool.

Jessie uncurled her fists and smoothed out imaginary wrinkles on the front of her suit. Looking down, she could see straight to her toes, with no enticing curves blocking her view.

Little boy, huh? We'll see about that Miss Nose Ring. Jessie smiled a little as she thought about reaching up and ripping the little gold ring out of Amanda's perfectly shaped nose.

They'd probably make me pay for the plastic surgery repairs.

Jessie glanced over her shoulder and watched Amanda gingerly pick up an empty potato chip bag between two perfectly manicured nails and daintily drop it in the trash bag.

I hope a lizard jumps out and runs up her arm.

For a split second, Jessie smiled at the image, and then she sighed.

Just my luck she'd have every boy over there to protect her.

Her chest tightened. An ache pulled at the back of her neck.

My head hurts.

She hated the feeling right before sobering up after a good high. It was so depressing. Her head was buzzing and she could feel the start of a headache forming. Amanda's interruption didn't help, either. Tears welled up in her eyes.

Life sucks.

"Hey, Jessie, come here."

Jessie turned toward the pool to see John coaxing a group of stoned teenagers out of the pool.

"Be right there," she called back. Using the back of her hand, she wiped at her face. Normally, she didn't let Amanda's comments bother her so much. *It must be the stupid mood I'm in tonight,* she thought.

Dragging her feet, Jessie made her way over to the side of the pool where John was threatening a tall skinny boy with a painful wedgie if he didn't get out of the pool immediately.

"They're just laying there like a bunch of floating logs." Jessie said as she stood next to John.

"More like a bunch of floating turds."

Jessie cupped her hands around her mouth like a megaphone and yelled, "All right, you slackers! Get your butts out of the water now. It's time to go home."

"Thanks, Jess," John said dryly. "I could have done that."

"Yeah? Then why'd you call me over to help?"

"I dunno, wait ... oh, yeah, I remember now." John slapped his forehead. "Can you get all the trash out of the pool?"

"Well," Jessie leaned back to look up at John and drawled with a big grin on her face. "I dunno, some of that trash looks too big to fit in a garbage bag."

Confused, John looked at Jessie with a blank expression then burst out laughing when he finally understood her sarcastic remark. "You think you're so funny, dontcha? A regular Jerry Seinfield." He gently pushed Jessie from behind toward the pool. "You just pick up the real garbage, I'll take care of the floating turds."

Jessie laughed and skipped away to get the long handled net to scoop out the cups, bags, and other party garbage the celebrating teenagers carelessly threw in the pool.

Methodically, Jessie dipped the net into the pool and filled it with trash, let the water drain, then emptied the net in a pile on the pool deck. At first, it was hard to avoid accidentally bumping into the other kids with the net, but as she continued, she discovered it was necessary sometimes to give one of the kids a whack just to motivate them to get out of the pool.

Lazy bunch of bums.

By the time she got to the deep end, most of the kids had groggily vacated the pool. Jessie looked down and saw Robbie gripping the edge of the pool, struggling to stay afloat.

"Come on out, Robbie."

"I'm gonna sleep here tonight," the skinny, olive-skinned boy responded grumpily.

Jessie poked him with the pool net, forcing him to lose his balance and go under water.

"Hey," Robbie sputtered as he resurfaced. "What's the big idea?"

"It's time to get out of the pool, let's go." Jessie swished the net threateningly close again.

"Okay, okay. Why don't you get Anna out too?" Robbie pointed to the last person left floating in the water.

Jessie sighed.

What am I, the designated babysitter?

"She's next. Just get out and help clean up, okay Robbie?"

Robbie splashed indignantly at Jessie but obediently swam to the shallow end and crawled out of the pool.

"Yo, Anna," Jessie called to her friend. "Come on, it's time to get out. You're gonna look like a wrinkled old prune."

Jessie scooped the last of the trash out of the pool and turned to lend Anna a hand.

Anna hadn't moved.

Jessie laid the pool net down on the deck and knelt close to the edge.

"Anna!" she shouted.

Jessie reached a hand out to tap Anna on the arm. Still no response. With shaking fingers, Jessie grasped Anna's arm and tried to pull her closer to the side of the pool.

Slick with water, Anna's arm slipped away.

"Hey, John! Robbie! Somebody! Help me!" Jessie's voice quivered with apprehension.

Chapter Two

Jessie screamed Anna's name and plunged feet first into the water next to her friend. Reaching out, she grabbed Anna's arm to pull her toward the side of the pool.

"Anna. Anna!" Jessie screamed as she shook the girl's arm hard. Jessie felt the coldness of Anna's skin seep through her trembling fingers.

Oh, God. No.

She turned her over. No quick giggle burst from her pouting blue lips and no mischievous smile appeared on her still babyish pale face.

Jessie drew in a sharp breath, her chest squeezing with the effort. She turned to the group that had gathered at the side of the pool and babbled incoherently, "Anna ... she's not breathing ..."

With one voice, the group gasped. Shock rippled across their faces. Disbelief echoed through the crowd.

Jessie felt herself becoming disconnected from what was happening. Her world crashed into disjointed scenes and unfolded in front of her. She was no longer a part of the scene but observing it from a distance. She drifted backwards then upwards, spiraling higher away from the crowd.

Mentally shaking herself, Jessie forced herself into action. She pulled and lifted Anna's body. "Help me get her out of the water. Hurry."

Hands reached out tentatively to grasp Anna's cold body. In the distance, Jessie heard someone yell for Mike while others surrounded her asking a billion questions. What's going on?" What's the matter with Anna?" "Is she okay?" "Did she pass out?"

"Get back!" Jessie screamed to force the others to back up and give her some room. She turned fearful eyes to John and begged him to call 911.

Turning to a girl standing next to him, John said quickly, "Kristie, go to the payphone next to the rec room and call 911."

Pounding feet sounded on Jessie's left. She watched as Mike ran straight for them, screaming Anna's name.

"Mike, Mike, hurry." Jessie called out to him.

"Jessie! Get up. Get up now!" John pulled at Jessie's arm just as

Mike launched himself forward and painfully slid along the pool deck to Anna's side. If Jessie hadn't moved, Mike would have slammed his body into hers.

Mike yanked Anna's arm, pulling her up into his lap. Anna's head lolled to one side, her arms limply fell behind her.

"OH GOD! Anna, wake up!" Mike cried as he shook her. Anna's head swung back and forth, her wet hair clinging to her face and shoulders.

John wrapped his arms around Jessie and pulled her clear of the action. Collapsing in his arms, she watched in horror as Mike clumsily attempted to give Anna CPR. It looked more like he was kissing her rather than actually trying to save her life. Tears rolled down her cheeks as they all stood helplessly watching Mike beg Anna to wake up.

Unable to stand on her own, Jessie used John for support. Transfixed by the horrific scene in front of her, she barely felt the bumps and shoves as she was jostled left and right by scrambling teenagers while they crowded in and out of the scene.

Through tears, Jessie looked down at Anna, hoping she would make some movement. That she would start breathing. But she didn't move at all. All she did was lay there. Mike screamed out, "Anna, stop messing around!"

Anna didn't open an eye. He slapped her face, pulled her arm, then blew into her mouth. Nothing. Panic set in among the crowd. Disjointed voices rolled across the night air.

"Go call an ambulance!"

"I gotta get outa here."

"Somebody already did!"

"This is bad ... you think we'll get in trouble?"

One by one, as if secretively choreographed, the teenagers disappeared. Each one, suddenly discovering that they had some place to be in a hurry.

Silently, Jessie watched them leave. She figured that most of them took off because they didn't need any trouble with the cops. She figured the others were afraid of being caught with alcohol or drugs. *Cowards, they probably just don't want to get involved.*

Then she heard a siren wailing in the distance and an urgency coursed through her. Her arm jerked sideways. She looked over to find John pulling on her arm; pulling her away from the crowd. Stunned, she let him lead her away from the pool area as the sirens screamed louder.

The muted sound of a person running on the grass behind her caught her off guard and she stumbled. Another teenager disappeared into an apartment to her left. Jessie looked back one last time to see the last of the teenagers gather their belongings and slip away into the darkness.

Chapter Three

Barefoot, Jessie stood on the patio of John's second floor apartment. A little shiver ran up her spine. The sun, barely above the horizon, streaked the pearl gray sky with luminescent pinks and blues mixing into yellows and oranges. The humidity rose from the ground in foggy patches, giving her an overhead view of fallen clouds. *It's going to be hot again today.*

Birds sang and squirrels chirped quietly in deference to the gloom of the previous night's events. With puffy, swollen eyes, she peered into the trees and could just make out the pool area below. *I'll never see the pool in the same way again.*

Hands trembling, Jessie fluffed her fingers through her short hair. The pounding in her head that had finally subsided enough for her to move returned in full force. Her hands clung to the sides of her face in agony. A pain-filled moan escaped her lips as she squeezed her eyes shut hoping to shut out the headache too. *What happened last night?*

With shaking hands, she lit a cigarette from the half crumpled pack on the patio table and sat in one of the faded plastic chairs. She blew a cloud of smoke into the air and watched it float away among the clutter of dwarf palm trees and tropical plants John's mother scattered about the patio in an attempt to gain some privacy.

Judging by the lack of activity among the other apartment dwellers and the dawning sky, Jessie assumed it was still too early to call her mom. She seriously doubted that her mom even knew what happened yet. Tears fell unchecked down her cheeks. Sighing deeply, Jessie dismally thought to herself, *"I don't even know what happened."*

Leaning forward, she pushed a potted plant of climbing ivy out of the way, rested her elbows on the wood railing, and let her chin sink into her hands. Sniffling, she looked out at the empty pool.

After John dragged her away, she had spent the most of last night just sitting in the same chair watching the chaotic activities below. All was quiet now. *Oh, Anna.*

The crowds were gone. One forgotten end of yellow police tape was still left tied to a pool chair. Its trailing end fluttered in the morning breeze. The rest of the pool chairs were overturned and piled haphazardly in one corner, pushed hastily out of the way to make room for the stretcher.

When she closed her eyes she could still see the red and blue flashing lights from the emergency vehicles pulsing the night sky. In her mind, she could again hear the scratchy disconnected radio voices drifting across the grounds. The distance between her safe position high above the crowd, behind the barrier of trees and the pool wasn't much, but she could have been a million miles away.

With unchecked tears streaming down her face, she had mutely watched. By the time the paramedics arrived, the pool area was deserted.

No one was left to explain. The only evidence of recent activities was overturned tables and chairs, scattered plastic cups, and empty chip bags.

Everyone else had disappeared. Almost everyone. Everyone except Mike. He had sat like a stone statue, weeping on the cold, wet pool deck, cradling Anna's lifeless body to his chest.

Click.

Jessie jumped. She turned to look through the patio door and saw that John had switched on the television. A commercial about cat litter was just ending. Then she heard it. Her back stiffened. She shoved her hands into the front pockets of her cutoffs and tried hard to not stare at the television.

The report began, "Seventeen year old, Anna Jane Marshall, who graduated this year from Bridgeway High school, died in an apparent drowning accident. She was pronounced dead early this morning around 3:45 a.m. According to the Bridgeway police report, when the ambulance and paramedics arrive, she had been dead for at least an hour."

"Early medical examination reports indicate the death was presumed to be by drowning although the investigation into possible drug and alcohol abuse continues." The reporter turned to the officer seated at the news desk to her right. "Officer Bailey, would you like to make a statement?"

"Yes, thank you." Officer Bailey turned to the camera. "Our preliminary investigation shows that Anna was with a group of teenagers participating in what appeared to be an unauthorized, impromptu graduation party at a local apartment complex. Apparently, drugs and alcohol were being used, probably obtained illegally. We need your cooperation in helping us find the rest of the teenagers involved. If you saw anything or heard anything, please contact the police department at 555-TIPS. Your call will be held in confidence and you may remain anonymous."

Grim-faced, Officer Bailey turned back to the news reporter, indicating he was finished with his statement. "Thank you, Officer Bailey." She patted his arm and smiled gently into the camera, "Again, that number is 555-TIPS. Remember, anything you report is confidential."

The camera switched views and pre-recorded video of the local high school's graduation ceremony filled the screen. An off-screen voice droned on about Anna's high school accomplishments and how a college in California had recently accepted her application. The video ended with the yearbook photo of Anna and the dates 1982 - 1999 beneath the picture.

The television reporter promised to return with more surprising teenage death statistics after the commercial break.

Click.

"What are we going to do?" Jessie whispered to John as he turned off the television and took the lit cigarette from Jessie's unsteady fingers.

"Nothing."

"What do you mean 'nothing'?"

"Dammit! Jessie! What can we do?"

"Can't we go talk to somebody?"

"No matter who we talk to or what we say, we'll get in trouble." John paced back and forth across the carpeted living room smoking in jerky motions. "We had booze. Drugs. Shit, we're all underage."

"But ..."

"No, let's just wait and see what happens."

"But, Anna—"

"She drowned, Jessie. It was an accident. That's all. Let it blow over. Just ... wait." He held the cigarette between two fingers and sucked hard. He gave Jessie a long direct look then handed the cigarette back to her.

Jessie noticed a stiffness about John that made him look years older than eighteen. She saw a familiar look in his eyes that reminded her of the times he would come over to her house after his mother returned home from a night out of heavy drinking. Jessie knew there was no use in arguing with him. He had made up his mind. She would follow his lead. She always did.

She walked back out on the patio and crushed out her cigarette. Absently, she lit another one, drawing a shaky breath as she did. *It's going to be all right. It's going to be all right.* She repeated the words in her mind hoping to block out all other thoughts.

A melodic tone chirped from her backpack. Her pager. At almost the exact same time, the telephone rang. John and Jessie stared at each other.

"No one ever calls this early," John whispered.

"Maybe it's your mom?" Jessie whispered back, trying to be positive. She went to pick up her backpack and see who paged her.

"Yeah, right," John rolled his eyes, "and maybe last night was all just a bad dream, too."

Jessie clutched her stomach, her backpack forgotten. She hugged her slender waist with both arms. Images of Anna's lifeless body float-ing in the water flashed before her brimming eyes. *I wish it all had been a bad dream.*

John reached for the telephone and then saw Jessie's reaction. He picked up the cordless telephone and gave Jessie quick hug at the same time. "Hello?"

"Hey." John put his hand over the mouthpiece and whispered to Jessie, "It's RJ."

Nodding that she heard him, Jessie walked back out to the patio. The sun was completely up and so were some of the neighbors. From her vantage point above, she could see people moving around in the closer apartments. A baby's cry competed with children's laughter while a car door slamming resounded from the parking lot.

Two little boys about seven years old ran across the lawn and headed for the pool dragging their towels behind them in the grass. She watched as they rattled the locked gate back and forth trying to force it open.

The management must have locked it last night.

With nervous hands, Jessie rubbed impatiently at the collar of her t-shirt, pulling it out and running her fingers inside trying to loosen it.

Why is it so hard to breathe?

Needing a distraction, she headed back into the apartment and turned on the television with the remote control. Slouching back on the sofa, she lowered the volume so that she didn't disturb John's conversation on the telephone.

The news was back on. A reporter sited statistics with graphs and bar charts on the video screen behind her, while another reporter added commentary.

"... leading cause of death among adolescents ages fifteen to twenty-four in Florida is unintentional injury, including drowning."

The second reporter asked, "What about the United States statis-tics, Karen?"

Karen responded, "Well, Jim, It's also the leading cause of ado-lescents in the United States. At least one adolescent, between the ages of 10 to19 years old, dies of an injury every hour of every day; about 15,000 die each year."

Jim consulted his notes then asked, "What about diseases? Don't they have a high rate?"

Karen shook her head and said, "Injuries kill more adolescents than all diseases combined. For every injury death, there are about 41 injury hospitalizations and 1100 cases treated in emergency depart-ments."

"We've heard so much about violence among adolescents, where do those statistics fit in, Karen?"

A new graph appeared behind the reporters as if on perfect cue.

Karen answered, "Unintentional injury accounts for around 60% of adolescent injury deaths, while violence, such as homicide and suicide, accounts for the remaining 40%."

Jessie frowned at the television, more annoyed with the obvious lack of concern on the reporters' faces rather than the alarming numbers she just heard.

In a fit of disgust, Jessie hit the off button on the remote and threw it down on the sofa cushion beside her.

"Thanks, RJ, I'll let ya know." John's voice carried from the kitchen. He was standing at the counter buttering toast and balancing the telephone under his chin as he talked. Motioning to the toast, he mimed asking Jessie if she wanted a piece.

Jessie shook her head. She couldn't imagine eating anything right now. She figured it was just because she felt sick to her stomach from having a hang over, but in the back of her mind she doubted that was the only reason.

"Yeah. Bye." John laid the telephone on the counter and finished making his toast by adding huge globs of grape jelly.

"That was RJ."

"Yeah, I know, you told me before." Jessie moved over a bit on the sofa to give John some room.

"He says that the cops are pulling in kids from the party last night and anyone who lives around here." He took a huge bite of toast and said between chews, "asking lots of questions."

"Like what?"

"Like if there was a party last night, who was there, was there any drinking, drugs, that sorta stuff." John licked his fingers free of jelly and started on the next piece.

Jessie turned and looked directly at John with an expression of exasperation. "And ... ?"

"And ..." John continued with a small display of dramatics, "most kids are denying there was a party. No one's admitting to using drugs or even drinking. Pretty much everyone is just keeping their mouths shut."

He finished the last of his toast and glanced over at Jessie. "Look, Jess," he said, "most everyone there last night was just letting loose from getting through graduation. We're all going away to college in the fall. No one wants to start out with a record." He coughed and added, "Or in my case, add to it."

"Yeah, I guess so. But, Anna ..."

John grabbed Jessie's upper arms and shook her a tiny bit to get her attention. "Jessie," he began slowly, speaking very deliberately. "Anna is dead. It was an accident. An accidental drowning. We can't help her." He looked into Jessie's eyes. "But we can help ourselves," he continued in the same slow, quiet voice. "We have to help ourselves."

"Okay." Jessie replied.

John stared at Jessie while he gripped her arm tight. "I'm serious Jessie," he repeated. "We have to take care of each other."

"Uh... Okay..."

"Okay?"

"Yeah. Okay. I get it." Jessie pushed John's hand away. "Jeez, it's not like anybody killed her." She slumped back on the sofa and slammed her hand hard on the cushion. "An accident. Like you said." Punctuating each sentence with a slam, she continued, "Just a stupid," Slam. "freakin'" Slam. "acci—"

Keys rattled at the door, startling them.

"—dent ..." Jessie's voice trailed off as they waited for the door to open.

After much fumbling and more keys rattling, the door finally opened and John's mother stumbled through on unsteady legs.

She waved at the two of them on the sofa, mumbled "hi, kids," and lurched toward the hall to her room.

Jessie wrinkled her nose at the odor of stale beer, cheap perfume, and dried vomit that drifted past.

"Mom, I gotta tell—"

"Tell me later, I gotta get some sleep." The bedroom door slammed.

John turned to Jessie and shrugged his shoulders. "My mom's home," he said dryly.

"I better go." Jessie gathered her backpack and the rest of her belongings and headed for the door.

"Call me, okay?"

"Yeah, I will. I gotta get. My mom is probably wondering where I am by now." She pulled John down and gave him a long hug. Kissing him lightly on the cheek she said, "thanks for letting me stay last night."

"No problem. You know you always have a place here."

"Thanks." Jessie pulled open the door and stood awkwardly in the doorway. "I better hurry, so I can catch the bus."

"Umm ... let me know if you hear anything."

The telephone rang again in the background.

"I will." Jessie looked toward the kitchen where John had left the telephone. "You better get that before it wakes up your mom."

"Yeah. Well, see ya." John kissed Jessie briefly on the cheek then stepped back to close the door.

Slowly, Jessie stepped away from the door so John could close it. She walked down the stairs and out into the sun. Squinting, she let her eyes adjust before continuing down the sidewalk that led her under the patio of John's apartment. She shuffled her feet, not in as much of a hurry as she thought she was to get home. Passing John's apartment, she heard his voice, "This is John ..."

Overcome with curiosity, she stopped and listened. John's voice carried through the open patio door.

"Yes, sir, I can be there today."

"Yes, sir."

"No, sir."

"Thank you, sir."

"Good-bye."

All was quiet. To her left, someone turned on a radio. On her right, she could hear dishes being clanked together as if someone was loading a dishwasher.

Life goes on. They probably don't even know what happened only a few feet from their sleeping beds.

She trudged to the corner and sat on a bench to wait for the local bus. While she waited, she absently searched her backpack for her bus pass.

Her fingers closed over her pager. She had forgotten that it had gone off while she was at John's house. Popping a stick of gum in her mouth, she pulled the pager out of her backpack and punched up the last call. A cold vise squeezed around her heart. She couldn't breathe.

Her home telephone number.

Oh, shit, I'm in trouble.

Jessie gasped for air. Mrs. Marshall had to know what was going on because otherwise they wouldn't have released Anna's name on the news this morning.

If my mom's paging me, then that means she's heard the news too, and knows I didn't spend the night at Anna's. God, I'm in so much trouble.

The bus pulled up with a screech of brakes and cloud of black diesel exhaust, while Jessie struggled with her thoughts. Gathering her stuff, she blindly boarded the bus and hurried to the sit in the back, away from the other passengers. The hydraulic whoosh of the doors closing didn't faze her. The loud rumble and whine of the engines as the driver switched gears and headed down the road went unnoticed.

All she could hear was Mike's screams for Anna to wake up. All she could see was Anna's pale face, and her bluish lips, and her lifeless eyes staring back at her when she turned her body over in the water.

All she could think about was this was not how the best summer of her life was supposed to start.

Chapter Four

Footsteps echoed loudly on the polished ceramic tile floor as Katherine Marshall wandered aimlessly from room to room in the empty house. No forgotten television blared from the family room. No stereo blasting barely discernable lyrics pounded a heavy bass beat into her temples.

The pounding came from deep inside. Her head throbbed.

Up all night, she refused to take the pills the doctor gave her when she left the hospital early that morning.

My poor baby.

The police had wanted to send a grief counselor home with her so she wouldn't be alone.

What a funny thought. A counselor for a counselor.

Katherine almost smiled at the joke then caught herself before her lips could curve upward. Now was not a time for jokes. She knew there were things to do, people to call, papers to sign, funeral arrangements to make, but for some reason she couldn't figure out which to do first, so she did nothing. Just walked the empty halls of her home, going from room to room, in a slow, methodical motion.

Alone. Alone. I'm alone.

The words repeated in her mind with each footstep, causing a cadence for her to keep step with, a mantra for her to recite so she didn't have to think.

As she passed tastefully decorated windows, her eyes barely registered that the morning had finally dawned. That the darkness faded away.

Last night is over.

Usually, she relished sleeping in on a Saturday morning. But, not this Saturday morning. Usually, she would be irritated by the early parade of landscaping vehicles rumbling into the neighborhood to raise the noise level a full thirty decibels while they mowed, edged, clipped, and blew every blade of grass within a ten-block radius.

She didn't even notice when the big blue truck and its loaded trailer stopped in front of her house.

Usually, the telephone would ring by this time with a sleepy Anna on the other end of the line mumbling a garbled good morning with her plans for the day and when she would be home.

The telephone was off the hook.

Anna wasn't going to call this morning.

Anna would never call again.

A cold hand squeezed Katherine's heart so hard she nearly stumbled. If she hadn't been walking so slow, she might have fallen.

She stopped in her tracks and lifted a shaking hand to her mouth to gnaw on another jagged nail that had already been bitten down to the quick.

Yesterday she had a manicure. She was meticulous about keeping a standing weekly appointment with her manicurist. Yesterday had been a normal day.

At least I thought yesterday was a normal day.

Katherine's nervous nail-biting stopped. She breathed a heavy sigh that took a great deal of effort. If she could just keep breathing, she might make it through today.

The effort to think and breath at the same time was too much. Katherine crumpled to the floor and laid her hot forehead on the cool tile. Absently, she followed the smooth outline of the tile with one finger, tracing the flat square over and over as she stared at nothing. A part of her knew that this behavior was not accomplishing the long list of tasks ahead of her. A part of her knew that she needed help. A part of her knew that she had done all this once before when her husband died five years ago. A part of her didn't care.

The biggest part of her just lost her little girl and knew there was nothing she could do to bring her back. That part of her was stronger. That part of her won the struggle for sanity. Nothing mattered anymore. There was no one left to be strong for. There was no one left to protect. There was no one left to protect her.

I don't want to do this again. Please, God, don't make me go through this torture again.

Katherine lay flat on the tile, pressing herself into the floor. She wished the floor would open up and swallow her entire body. Make her disappear. Make the whole world disappear. A roaring grew louder and louder until it filled her head with nothing but the reverberation of the noise.

Yes, take me away. Make it all just go away!

She tensed her body, waiting for a bottomless pit to appear below her. She waited for the bliss of oblivion to replace her pain. A big hole. A sinkhole right under her house.

Sinkholes weren't uncommon in Florida. Katherine vaguely recalled reading about a family that barely got out of their house alive before half of it disappeared into the ground. She breathed a sigh of relief. A sinkhole would be the perfect answer to her prayers.

The roaring diminished. No trembling, ground-shattering chasm splintered the soft, beige stones. No stomach lurching drop into abysmal free-fall. She still lay on the cold tile of her empty house. Discernable now, the noise swept by the window and across the yard at a steady pace. Back and forth. Loud then faint.

A lawnmower.

Katherine pushed herself up to her knees. She didn't notice that her soiled blouse rode high on her waist. She didn't even hear or feel the snap and crack of bones and tendons forced to move too quickly. She only peered out the window to verify the sound of an actual lawnmower and not nature's timely answer to her pleadings.

There it was, circling her front lawn. The landscaper standing behind the large machine effortlessly guiding it as it floated across the lawn, cutting and spewing green confetti into the air.

No. No. "No!" She stumbled and tripped as she hurried to the front double doors and swung them both wide open.

Bright, warm sunlight dared to caress her face, making her swollen eyes squint. Birds sang. The smell of freshly mowed grass assaulted her stuffy nose. How dare life continue.

"Stop!" Katherine waved her arms frantically trying to get the man's attention over the deafening noise. "Stop! Go away!"

What the hell was his name? Mick? Rick? Nick? Nick!

Katherine cupped her hands around her mouth and screamed Nick's name.

Chapter Five

Nick Mancuso sang along with Santana about how hot it was so close to the sun, thinking that seven inches from a mid-day sun was probably a good description of how it always felt in Florida in the summertime. He squinted eyes, darkly shaded by wrap around sunglasses, toward the east. Not mid-day yet, but already hot.

He stood tall as he whirled the lawnmower efficiently, his tanned arms straining to keep the mower in a straight line. The headphones he used were large and bulky but they did their job by filtering out most of the deafening mower noise and retaining the more pleasant sounds. The upbeat music helped him get into a rhythm while keeping the monotony of running the machine over lawn after lawn to a minimum. He pretended to be a kind of conductor, using music to choreograph his cutting motions. It made time fly.

This is the life.

He loved the outdoors in Florida. There was no other place like it in the world. If he could, he'd spend his entire life outdoors. But, unfortunately, polite society required him to make a few concessions. One of which was keeping a job so that he could afford the necessary shelter and other survival amenities that held him just this side of vagrancy. He compromised his insatiable need for the outdoors only to teach biology at a small private school. During the summers, he cut lawns more for his greedy need to stay in shape and outside than for the actual income.

Landscaping businesses were as common as pelicans on the pier in this area. He was good at his job, an amiable employee, and kept to himself. He had a good reputation among the local businesses for being dependable. It worked out great for everyone.

He tapped his steel-toe, boot-covered foot as he kept time with the music all the while thinking that if he continued on the schedule he was on so far, he'd be done before noon and would have the rest of the day to go to the beach and catch some rays.

Then he saw her.

Oh shit, look what the cat dragged in.

With a touch of a button, all was silent. The machine coasted to a stop. With practiced grace, Nick set the brake and jumped off while removing his headphones and sunglasses at the same time to let them dangle around his neck. He mopped his sweating face with a handkerchief and gaped, awe-struck, at the crazed woman running toward him. He almost stepped backwards, thinking she was going to run right into him before she skidded to a stop just inches from his sweating body. Nick could see the dark circles that shadowed her eyes.

Mrs. Marshall?

The usually composed person who lived in this house was not the person who now stood in front of him waving her arms frantically and screaming at the top of her lungs. This woman looked years older with her face smeared with dried makeup and hair practically standing on end.

"Mrs. Marshall ...?"

"Get out of here!"

"Uh ... isn't this is our scheduled day, Mrs. Marshall? Did we make a mistake?" Nick hurried to his truck to check his clipboard wanting to be anywhere but close to an incoherent wild woman.

What a whack-job.

Most of the time he usually ignored the eccentric behaviors of his customers, but not when they were acting like Mrs. Marshall; he couldn't just dismiss her actions.

This is just too weird.

For all he knew, she could have a gun in the pocket of her tailored wrinkled slacks and start shooting him! All because he might have cut her lawn on the wrong day? Every day people ended up shot for a lot less than that.

I should have known something would happen to ruin a perfectly good day.

He slowly walked back to where she stood in the middle of the yard, making irritated, impatient movements, motioning him to return.

She ran shaking fingers through her hair making it stand even more on end. "Look, I don't care if it's the right day or not, just go away."

Stay calm, don't argue with her.

Nick kept his eyes on his clipboard so he wouldn't be caught staring at her stained silk blouse, buttoned incorrectly and half tucked up under her exposed bra strap. Inwardly cringing, he struggled to maintain a professional demeanor while he discreetly dialed his boss' number on his cellular phone.

"Umm ... Mrs. Marshall, maybe I can call my supervisor so he can talk to—"

"You're not calling anyone, you hear?" Katherine's voice rose higher ending in a pitch that would make most dogs come running.

Nick jumped. His fingers missed their cue and hit a seven instead of five. He quickly looked up, catching a glimpse of glazed, blood-shot eyes.

I really don't need this shit.

He couldn't believe that she was drunk at this hour. But, all the signs were there. He knew them so well. He thought he had seen enough to last a lifetime. Apparently not.

The erratic behavior, incoherent babbling, disheveled appearance, and misdirected anger brought back all the hurt and anger he had thought he had forgotten. His ex-wife had put him through two years of pure hell. A place he never wanted to visit again.

I really, really don't need this shit.

Nick forced his mind to clear. It wasn't his place to judge.

I'm not getting involved.

"Mrs. Marshall?" Nick spoke softly, not wanting to startle the woman who was staring off into the distance as if she couldn't remember why she was outside. He waited for her to acknowledge that she heard him. When she didn't, he continued anyway, "Mrs. Marshall? I'm going to go back to my truck and call my boss. Whatever the problem is, we'll get it straightened out. Okay?"

Not taking his eye off the wild-looking woman in front of him, he walked backwards. Sliding into the passenger seat, Nick caught his breath at the heat built up inside the cab of the truck. He threw his clipboard to the floor and quickly dialed his boss' cell phone.

Come on, man. Answer.

He pulled his headphones and sunglasses over his head and juggled the phone to keep from getting caught up in the tangle of wires and cord that kept him from losing his favorite work tools.

He had lost count of the number of rings in his ear when a shadow passed over him and a small tapping noise startled him so much that he nearly dropped the cell phone.

"Oh, shi—Mrs. Marshall!" Nick raked the fingers of his free hand through his hair, knocking the sweatband from his head. At the same time, he heard a faint "Dan, here." in his ear.

"Uh... Dan, got a situation here at the Marshall's."

"Yeah? Whazup?"

Nick glanced over at the woman standing so forlornly at the door of his truck. She was using the chipped nail of her index finger to pick at the dirt and grime caught in the seam between the door and the truck's body. She didn't look anything like the raving lunatic who screamed at him moments ago. Now, she just looked like a lonely, lost woman.

"Uh ... schedule mix-up, I think, hang on." Nick's eyes narrowed as he watched Mrs. Marshall's lips moving. She was saying something and he leaned over closer to hear.

"... can't fix it."

"Pardon?"

"... no one can fix this ..."

A roaring in Nick's ear forced him to pay attention to the man he had on hold. He could barely make out Dan's voice over the loud belching of a gas-powered hedger. Not even a telephone call could interrupt Dan from his intense schedule.

"Look, Nick. Gotta run. Take care of the Marshall thing. Let me know how it comes out. Later."

Nick looked down at the now silent cell phone in his hand.

Now what?

Disgusted, he threw the cell phone across the truck barely missing the stick shift as it bounced into the driver's seat, then turned his attention back to the woman who was methodically rubbing each water and dirt mark on his truck door with grubby fingers.

"Mrs. Marshall, if you want me to leave, then I'm going to leave. We'll come back another time, when you're more ... uhh ... umm ... when you're feeling better." He stumbled over his words, trying to maintain a diplomatic distance.

What am I supposed to say? When you're not drunk?

Nick waited a respectable period for Mrs. Marshall to agree that he should come back another time. While he waited, he leaned a little closer to her, trying to hear her mumbling words. He noticed that although her lips were dry and cracked, they were swollen and bruised like she had been biting them. Afraid of making eye contact, he glanced quickly upwards and realized her eyes were also swollen and red. Not from alcohol, like he first thought, but from crying. Instinct forced him to hold his breath, not wanting to breathe in the predictable sour smell he expected.

Oh, shit. I really stepped into it this morning.

Leaning back, Nick checked his watch and then took a deep breath that strained his t-shirt across his chest and let it out in resignation.

I always was a sucker for tears.

"Mrs. Marshall, would you like someone to talk to?"

Chapter Six

Katherine heard the gentleness in his tone before she actually comprehended his question. She lifted tear-stained eyes to his face and asked him what he said.

Nick repeated his question. "Would you like someone to talk to?"

Katherine opened her mouth to scathingly retort that it was none of his damn business whether she needed someone to talk to, but somehow the words that came out were different.

"My daughter died last night."

Katherine's eyes flew up to Nick's face. *My God, did I just say that?*

She saw shock registered on her yardman's face and knew that she had for the first time, spoken those words aloud.

Katherine raised a shaking hand to her forehead and brushed at stray hairs tickling her skin. Her fingertips touched her head, but she couldn't feel them. She pressed harder. A blackness clouded her eyes, starting on the edge of her sight and rushing inward, like the fog rolling onto the shore. *I never faint* was her last conscious thought before she felt strong arms catch her as she fell to the ground.

꙲ ꙳

Nick's instincts kicked into high gear even before the full impact of Mrs. Marshall's statement registered in his brain.

He held out his arms and caught her limp body. He lifted her slight weight into his arms, shifted her body until he was comfortable, and then strode purposely toward the front of the house and through the front door.

Nick felt a strong sense of déjà vu as he carried a passed-out woman in his arms. Expecting to smell the sour odor of old booze and sweat, his mind grasped on the small piece of knowledge that Mrs. Marshall wasn't drunk, nor had she been drinking at all. He smelled the faint remaining fragrance of an expensive perfume and only a whiff of body odor.

It's not the same. She's not the same.

Quickly assessing the inside foyer of Mrs. Marshall's expensive home, he made for the comfortable-looking sofa in the family room he could just see from where he stood.

After making sure she wasn't going to fall and hurt herself, Nick found a downstairs bathroom. He opened a cabinet and discovered it completely stocked with every first aid article imaginable. Making quick work of his tasks, he washed his hands then gathered towels, basin, and soap before making his way back to the still unconscious lady of the house.

Katherine felt soft, cool touches stroking her face. Calmed, her mind filtered the soothing sounds of comfort, even though she couldn't understand the words.

She hated to wake up. What a horrible nightmare. She tried to lift her head, but it felt heavy. She must have spent the entire night fighting against inconceivable situations but couldn't remember much of it. She only knew that right now all was serene. Turning her head slightly, she snuggled deeper into the softness trying to comprehend why the tile was no longer cold or hard.

She smiled slightly, as she drifted in between the waking world and dreamers. She must have fallen into the abyss that opened in her floor and landed somewhere soft. She sighed pleasantly.

What a nice place. So quiet.

Against her desires, Katherine felt herself being pulled out of her dream. Someone was calling her name. She pushed away from the sound.

"Mrs. Marshall ...?"

"Mrs. Marshall, please wake up."

Her eyes fluttered, then squinted shut at the bright light. Using her hand, she shielded her faced from the glaring sunlight and felt the pillow beneath her head.

I'm not on the floor. If I'm not on the floor, where am I?

Before opening her eyes, Katherine took a deep breath to steady her racing heart. Something happened and she needed to gather her thoughts and think it through.

What was the last thing you remember, Katherine?

Floor. Cold tile. Noise. Sinkhole. Window. Lawn.

Lawnmower! That's it.

Katherine's eyes flew open and she winced at the pain from the light. Steadying herself, she pushed upwards and tried to get into a sitting position. Before she could even finish pulling herself up, she felt strong arms around her shoulders and waist and more pillows tucked behind her head.

Katherine gasped.

"Mrs. Marshall. I'm sorry for startling you. Umm ... you see, you umm ... fainted."

"I ... fainted?" she gestured impatiently. "I don't faint."

Nick grinned. "Well, ma'am, you sure did this time."

"Mr. Uhh ... Nick, is it?"

"Nick."

"Yes, Nick. Well," Katherine fumbled with her clothing, trying to straighten and tuck discreetly. "I appreciate you coming to my aid. I've had a very stressful evening." She looked about the room, noticing for the first time that the drapes had been open to let in the light.

"Mrs. Marshall, if you don't mind my saying so," Nick said in a halting tone, "I think, maybe, you should call, ummm ... someone."

"Young man, I don't—" Katherine returned sharply, then softened her tone as she saw the hurt look in this nearly complete stranger's eyes. She rarely said more than a sentence or two whenever he mowed the lawn, if she was home at the time. He knew nothing about her situation, but he was willing to help. He didn't deserve her anger. She began again, "I'm sorry, please forgive me." She held out her hand and touched the one that held the damp washcloth. "Thank you. For this." Then she took the cloth from his hand.

Twisting the damp cloth between her fingers, she hesitated, then rushed forward as new tears fell down her cheeks, "My daughter died last night. An accident. Drowning accident."

With her head bowed and tears warping her vision, she sensed more than saw Nick cover her hand with his.

Her shoulders shook as sobs wracked her body. She cried through her pain. She cried through her hurt. She cried through her grief. Through it all, she clung to Nick's hand.

Nick let the older woman cry until she was drained. When she fell into an exhausted sleep, he extricated his numb hand from her grip and stood to stretch the kinks from his cramped legs. He shook his hand to try and restore circulation as he paced the length of the large room.

What the hell am I getting myself into?

Unknowingly, he traced almost the exact same path Katherine had blazed in the early hours. He didn't notice the tasteful decorations, but he did notice the hall phone had been taken off its hook. Without thinking, he placed the receiver back in its cradle.

Nick jumped as the telephone rang immediately. It's shrill, sharp tone echoing loudly in the tiled hall. Instinctively, he snatched it up, not wanting it to wake up Mrs. Marshall.

"Marshall residence."

Nick waited for the caller to identify themselves but he only heard a sharp intake of breath on the other line so he asked, "May I help you?"

The caller's heavy breathing was the only response Nick got to his repeated question.

"Stupid jerk."

Nick wasn't sure if his thoughtless comment was directed at the anonymous caller or himself.

Awkwardly, Nick replaced the receiver, doubting whether it had been a good idea to pick up the telephone at all and vowed to let it ring next time.

I'm not going to get involved. She must have an answering machine or something like that. I can't hang around and take messages for her.

Nick walked back into the room where Katherine slept and stood at the end of the sofa. Without the harsh sun and her anger, her face was softer, younger. She didn't look nearly as old as he thought, although even being generous, she was still at least fifteen years older than him.

You're not so bad after all, Mrs. Marshall. You just might be one of the greatest ladies I know. I hope you make it through this.

Nick covered Mrs. Marshall with a small throw taken from the back of a chair, wrote a short note, and then left quietly.

He loaded his equipment into his truck and trailer then called his boss on the cell phone to let him know he was taking the rest of the day off and headed for the nearest newsstand to buy a morning paper.

Chapter Seven

Sergeant Torrence Robles picked up a paper napkin from the pile on the table and wiped his perspiring forehead. *Too damn humid already*, he thought.

Twisting his wrist around to check the time, he added two more names and crossed one name off the list that was paper clipped to a file folder in front of him. If the interviews kept up this way, he'd end up with more names left on the list than he started with.

There had to be an easier way to find the core group. These kids had more stories than a ten-year old with Pokémon trading cards.

He shuffled through the pile of papers and found the file he was looking for—Springwater Apartment Complex. Sgt. Robles skimmed the list of complaints called into the police department over the last few years.

He whistled low under his breath. He knew it was going to be a long list. The complex had a reputation for renting to "undesirables."

Last night's accident would be just one more reason for the community to petition to have it shut down. The property the apartment complex claimed was just on the edge of the city limits and only declared city status by a small loophole in the city ordinance.

Just last week, Sgt. Robles read in Charles Beckett's newspaper column that the city council had been working for over six months to find some way to change the ordinance and re-map the city limits. Even though it meant losing the square footage, they felt it was worth it considering the reputation of the apartment complex.

Typical solutions for politicians. They'd rather just let someone else deal with the problem, than acknowledge it was an issue of their city.

Sgt. Robles flipped through the rest of the file, mentally noting the names of those with the most complaints logged against them.

He noticed one or two family names that appeared over the years. That surprised him as the apartment complex was known for its transient community. People who rented those apartments didn't stay around long. Not over a year, from what he had seen. The city wasn't exciting enough for them. These people got bored easily and drifted whenever the mood hit them. Usually, they left just a step ahead of bill collectors.

He took out his PDA and made notes of those families that have been in the apartment complex for more than a year. Then he made a separate list of those names that made the complaint list more than three times. The third list was the most difficult to put together. He used the papers he had in front of him to start it.

He needed to make a list of all the families with teenagers between the ages of 15 and 19. Most families didn't list all the children because they were afraid that they would be charged extra. This list would take a little longer to compile and he would need information from a number of sources. His first stop was the apartment complex manager's office. That office changed managers almost as often as the tenants did. Getting their cooperation wouldn't be difficult, getting their trust was another issue.

The complex was part of his regular patrol. He spent a lot of time in the manager's office talking to the staff and evicting delinquent tenants.

It wasn't his favorite part of the job. But, then again, neither was dealing with a child's death.

Looking out the small, dusty window of the processing room, Sgt. Robles watched small feathery wisps of white clouds float carelessly in the brilliant blue sky.

It figures. Best day of the month, and I'm stuck inside with paperwork.

Not withstanding the weather, Sgt. Robles knew it was going to be a shitty day all around.

Chapter Eight

Eager to hit the beach and read the newspaper, Nick pulled his truck up to an island of newspaper vending machines and scanned the many colored boxes for the familiar brown and white logo of the *Bridgeway News*.

His coins sank with a lonely clank into the locked canister of the vending machine.

"Must have just missed the delivery," Nick thought absently as he pulled his paper off the top of the stack. The lid slammed closed with a loud bang that always made him pull his fingers back as if they were going to get caught in the vending lid.

Maneuvering through the parking lot to a vacant space, Nick put the truck in park, left the engine and air conditioning running, and hurriedly skimmed the local section of the paper.

Car accident on the interstate ... bar fight ... gun shot ... here it was ... drowning.

Nick read the short article quickly then read it a second time more slowly. There wasn't much information. From what he gathered from the little he read, some kids had a pool party, and the Marshall girl drowned.

Nick assumed that the reporter only gathered as much as he could from the police report to make the early morning edition.

Maybe tomorrow's paper will have more information.

Nick sped along the intercoastal highway to his favorite beach eager to put the whole morning behind him. Unfortunately, instead of the bright sky and blue water, all he saw was the image of Mrs. Marshall looking so sad and alone laying on her sofa.

He turned his truck into the nearest convenience store and headed for a payphone. He needed to talk to his Aunt Laura before he could put the morning truly behind him.

❧ ❧

Sgt. Robles wiped his sweating brow with a square of paper towel torn from a roll he kept in the front seat of his squad car. He had been knocking on doors and interviewing insolent teenagers and clueless parents all morning.

He checked his list and verified the address on the building.

4576 Apartment D. Here goes.

He knocked rapidly and firmly on the door then waited.

A small boy's head appeared at the narrow, beveled window next to the door and disappeared just as quickly.

Sgt. Robles grinned as he heard the sound of running feet fading down a short hallway inside the apartment. Most kids and adults too, had the same reaction when they saw his massive six and a half-foot, 250-pound frame bearing down on them.

He waited about thirty seconds and rapped on the door again, this time calling out a friendly hello along with his knock.

The door's chain rattled in its track before the doorknob turned. Sgt. Robles watched the door open slowly and waited patiently for the person inside to acknowledge him.

"Waddaya want?" mumbled a tossled-head sleepy young man. According to his notes he was twenty-one. If he hadn't known, he would have guessed he was about the age of eighteen.

The odor of dried sweat and bad breath floated through the opening of the door up to Sgt. Robles' sensitive nostrils. They flared in distaste. He looked through the door and quickly took in the smells and sights of a room that didn't look like it had been cleaned for months.

"Are you Paul Roman?"

"Who wants ta know?"

Sgt. Robles drew a deep breath, despite the dirty smells wafting from the apartment and lowered his voice. "Look, kid. We can do this one of two ways. You can either cooperate and drop the attitude and answer my questions the best you can, or we can go for a ride and the little guy here can take a trip to Child Protective Services."

Sgt. Robles smiled down at the small boy peeking out between the young man's legs, one thumb of a dirty hand in his equally dirty mouth.

Looking down at the little boy staring up at him adoringly the fight went out of him. "Alright, man. I don't need any trouble." He lifted the little boy in his arms, kissed him quickly and whispered in his ear then turned back to the policeman at his door. "Yeah, I'm Paul Roman."

Sgt. Robles took out his notebook and asked for identification. He copied down Paul's driver's license number. "Hey man, you need to get your address updated. This license isn't right."

"Yeah, okay." Paul mumbled and but his license back into his wallet.

Sgt Robles nodded towards the empty hall that led to the little boy's room. "Your kid?"

Paul turned as if he could still see the boy running towards his room. "Yeah. My son." His skinny chest swelled slightly with obvious pride. "He's four."

"The mother?"

"My girlfriend, she's at work right now."

"You work?"

Sgt. Robles watched Paul's eyes shift to the left and saw his Adam's apple spasmodically bob before answering.

"Yeah, sure. I work for a ... courier service."

"Courier Service? Which one?" His pen poised over his notebook.

"Uh ... just a local thing me and some friends do." He shifted from one foot to the other. "We, uh ... run errands for people, you know. Like, we go pick up stuff for people and bring it back."

Sgt. Robles wrote a few notes in his book then looked up expectantly. He learned that if he just waited, the person usually told him more than if he asked a bunch of questions. He watched Paul become uneasy and knew it was a matter of time.

"We do stuff for people, uh ... who can't. You know? Like ... like ... picking up groceries!" Triumphant, Paul blew his disgusting breath out.

Instinctively, Sgt. Robles backed up so that the offensive smell would drift away from him.

"You mean you run errands for little old ladies?" Sgt. Robles asked mockingly.

"Yeah, whatever. You know?" Paul hurried on, "Nuthin' illegal though."

"Right." Sgt. Robles changed tactics. "Were you running errands last night?" He put the emphasis on "running errands."

"Uh ... last night? Don't 'member, lemme think." Paul squinted his eyes and wrinkled his forehead as if he were trying to think very hard.

"Look, kid. Let me make it a little easier for you." Sgt. Robles would have laughed if he hadn't known he probably wouldn't get any answers after that. "Were you in the vicinity of this apartment complex's pool area between midnight and three this morning?"

"Pool area?"

"Yeah. The pool area."

"Here in this complex?"

"Yes, the pool in this apartment complex." Sgt. Robles gritted his teeth and took a firm grip of his pen as he hung on to his self-control.

"Uh, probably ... yeah, sure. I was there."

Sgt. Robles barely contained himself. He wanted to wrap his hands around this skinny kid's shoulders and shake some sense into him. He rolled his eyes upward and said a silent prayer for self-restraint.

"Did you make any deliveries to the pool last night?"

"Deliveries? Like what kind of deliveries?"

"You tell me. Did you take anything to the pool for anyone down there."

"Uh ... sure. Yeah. I took some kid a pack of cigarettes."

"Do you remember the kid's name?"

"No."

"Excuse me?" Sgt. Robles looked down at Paul with a hard gleam in his eye.

"Uh, maybe. I don't know." Paul nervously picked at the chipped paint on the doorjamb avoiding eye contact with the large policeman.

"Take a second to think about it, Paul." Sgt. Robles said softly. He leaned against the side of the building and casually flipped through his notebook, whistling under his breath, acting as if he had all the time in the world.

"Uh, he was a kid, you know. Like the all the other kids that hang out at the pool at night. They're always asking me to pick up stuff for them."

"And did you pick up something special that night for this kid?"

"Same stuff he always asks for, you know. Cigarettes. Stuff." Paul shuffled his feet, kicking at the bottom of the door jam.

"Ok, Paul. You remember taking some kid cigarettes, so, you had to remember what he looked like. Did he look like this kid?" Sgt. Robles opened his notebook and displayed a copy of a senior class picture from the school's yearbook.

Paul studied the picture for a long time. Sgt. Robles suspected the kid was just trying to stall. Hoping a story would pop into his head that he could tell.

Robles watched the little boy make his way back down the short hallway and wrap his arms around his daddy's leg. He used his leverage to nudge the kid again.

"Come on, Paul. Either you tell me here or I take you down to the station and you tell me there."

Paul's head snapped up. His body went rigid. "Take me down? For what? I didn't do nothing."

"Well, you've just admitted to buying cigarettes for under-age kids. That's a crime in this state, you know."

"Shi-"

"Watch your mouth." Sgt. Robles' attitude began to change. His voice hardened. "Look, I'm done playing with you. Either you talk or I pull you in. We've got a dead girl on our hands and I want to know if you were there or not, and if so, with whom?"

"I didn't do nuthin' to no girl. It wasn't even a girl who asked for the stuff. It was that kid. This one in the picture. Geez, give me a break, huh? I gotta kid myself. I don't need no trouble."

Paul pushed the picture back into Sgt. Robles' hands. He picked up his son and held him close to his chest.

Chapter Nine

Katherine sat on the cushioned window seat of the large bay window in her bedroom. She placed one hand on the cold pane and traced a tiny raindrop's path. Staring past the dark green of the closely clipped, thick-bladed St. Augustine grass, past the privacy fence, and over the other equally spaced houses in her neighborhood, Katherine could just make out the drawbridge over the intercoastal before the fog blanketed the rest from her view. She shivered and wrapped her arms around herself to not only give warmth, but a sense of being.

There's no one left. This must be what it feels like to be so completely alone. Please, God, please take me too.

With her head bent, she laid her hot forehead against the cool glass. The stark contrast of the cold numbed her skin as she wept.

The ringing of the telephone brought Katherine back to the present. She could hear her sister as she talked softly to whoever was on the telephone. It didn't matter who it was. Katherine wasn't speaking to anyone this morning.

Slowly, as if she were old and frail, Katherine pushed back from the window seat and stood. She knew it was time to get ready, but like the sun, she didn't want to make an appearance.

Standing in front of her full-length mirror, she looked at the woman staring back at her. She stood rigidly upright, awkwardly pulling down the hem of the simple black dress that clung to her slight body. The image all too familiar. She had worn the same dress five years ago. Today the hair was lighter, more gray, but other than that, she was the same.

But, I'm not the same, a voice inside her screamed.

She pinned the small black hat on her head and draped the wisp of netting across her face. After five years, she was doing it again, preparing for a funeral.

The similarities crossed over in Katherine's mind. She lost her place in the present and crumpled to the floor, unable to stop the flood of memories.

Oh, John, I miss you so much. How could this be happening? First you, now Anna. Please take me too. I can't live without the both of you. You were my life. We promised to be there for each other, always. Make it better, please. Bring back our old life. Come back to me.

Caught up in the past, Katherine didn't hear her sister's voice until she had called her name several times.

"Katherine? Oh, hon, here, let me help you finish dressing." Margaret put her arms under Katherine's shoulders and helped her sit up on the edge of the bed.

Katherine leaned into her older sister's enveloping arms and clung to her sturdy body. "Oh, God, Margaret, I don't know if I can do this."

"I know, hon, I know." Margaret gently rocked back and forth crooning to her younger sister. "You just lean on me. I'm here for you."

"I miss John."

"I know, darlin'. I know. We'll get through this together. You and me."

"I'm so glad you're here."

"Wild dogs wouldn't keep me from you, hon."

"What about Hank, and the kids, and ... ?"

"Now, you hush. Don't be worrying about them. They can take care of themselves. If I only did one thing right in this world, it was to raise my family to be self-sufficient."

"But, Sarah just had the baby, she needs you."

"Katherine, look at me." Margaret stopped rocking and held her grieving sister at arm's length.

Obediently, Katherine turned red, swollen eyes to meet her sister's more somber ones.

"You need me, right now. Sarah gave birth to two healthy boys already. I think she can handle this angel of a baby girl for a little while until grandma gets back." Margaret's eyes shined with maternal pride at her daughter's most recent accomplishment.

Katherine sniffed softly and leaned her head on her sister's shoulder. "Oh, Mags, I'll never know the joy of my daughter's first child."

Wrapping her arms around her sister's small frame, Margaret held her tightly against her ample bosom. She knew that at this moment, no words could bring the comfort Katherine desired.

Katherine's shoulders sagged and a torrent of tears fell over Margaret's chest. Margaret patted and rubbed her younger sister's back. She made soft shushing sounds and held her tightly. She let the stormy flood ebb and flow as Katherine hiccupped in between each wave of tears.

Oh, God, please watch over my children and my children's children. Please keep them safe and away from harm. Dear, God, please don't bring this kind of suffering to my house.

Margaret caught her breath. *Am I being selfish? Should I be praying for protection while my sister goes through this horror? Dear God, please know that I don't mean for my sister to suffer while I don't. Please, help ease my sister's suffering. Bring her comfort some-how. Help me to know what to say to her.*

Margaret's heart ached as she sat holding her sister and praying to God for respite.

"Katie-bug," Margaret whispered into her sister's hair. "There, there."

Humming softly, she rocked her sister gently, murmuring non-sense until Katherine's sobs ended in hiccups and the hiccups turned into soft sighs.

Margaret sensed a stiffening in her sister's body as she pulled herself back. Knowing it was time to back off, she straightened and smoothed Katherine's hair.

"There, now, Katie-bug," she crooned softly. "You had yourself a good cry. There's nothing wrong with that."

"Mags, you're the best. What would I do without you?"

"Well, now, let's not think about it, ok?"

Katherine sniffled, and then blew into the ever-present handker-chief. Wiping her nose, she even managed a half-hearted chuckle. "You haven't called me 'Katie-bug' in a long time." Katherine thought of all the times she had turned to her sister. A sister who was more like a mother than their own mother ever was, or ever could be.

Margaret patted her sister's hand, "you haven't been my 'Katie-bug' in a long time, hon."

"I know ..."

"Oh, now, don't go thinking about the past again. You can't change it. No matter, now." Margaret's chin rose a bit as she brushed imagi-nary lint from her sister's dress. Now was not the time for her to go into the whys and wherefores of her sister's career choice. Nor was it the time to try and get Katherine to admit she could have called their mother instead of her big sister.

"Come on now, let's have look at you." Squaring her shoulders, Margaret pushed nagging thoughts of absent parents and undisciplined children aside as she focused on her sister's needs.

Chapter Ten

Nick snapped open the morning newspaper and read the article heading again. "Services planned for teenager found dead in local pool." Once again he doubted his reasons for going to the memorial service for Anna Marshall. He continued to try and convince himself it was because he was paying his respect to a client.

If that's so true, then why can't you look at yourself in the mirror when you say it?

Disgusted with his cowardliness, he tossed the newspaper aside and pushed himself out of his truck before he changed his mind again.

Mindful of the traffic, he joined a group of pedestrians as they crossed the street and headed for the church.

❧ ❧

Impatient, Jessie pulled at John's arm. "Hurry up, man, we're gonna be late for the memorial service."

"Calm down, Jess." John said.

"But, look at all the cars already, we're gonna be the last ones in the church."

"No we're not." He glanced at his watch. "We've got plenty of time still. Just chill, ok?"

Exasperated, Jessie stuck out her tongue then resigned herself to walking sedately beside John along the wet, palm tree-lined path toward the church.

The church reigned high from a bluff overlooking the Gulf of Mexico. It's stark whiteness a beautiful, vivid contrast to the dark clouds and gray waters behind.

Sidestepping a puddle, Jessie looked up at John, "I'm glad the rain stopped. Although, somehow, it seemed right that it should rain today."

"Yeah, bad day for the beach." John responded absently.

"How can you think of going to the beach today of all days?" Jessie threw out her arms and whirled on John, catching him off guard.

"Huh? Whaddya mean? I was just thinking that you can't go to the beach on a rainy day, that's all. Jeez, Jess. Take it easy."

"I'm sorry, John. I'm not handling any of this very well." Jessie tucked her hand into John's and gave a little squeeze. "I'm scared."

"I know, kid."

Jessie looked up at John quickly. The tone in his voice hinted at more than his recent maturity by graduating high school. He seemed more distant, as if he had a huge weight on his shoulders.

He's worried too, I can tell. He just doesn't want to show it.

"Did you get grounded for not telling your mom the truth about where you were ... that night?" John couldn't bring himself to describe the night Anna died any other way.

"Yeah. But, I kinda feel like I deserved it, you know, in a way, because of what happened and all."

"Hey, at least you got to come here."

"Yeah, but I have to be back home right after."

John nodded. "How long you grounded?"

"I dunno, my mom's really pissed."

"I bet."

"Yeah, well I think she's just scared that it could have been me, you know?"

"Yeah, I guess." John muttered. He recalled how his own mother had reacted when he told her about the drowning and that he had to go down to the police station to give a statement. She had screamed at him for getting into trouble again and told him if he got arrested she wasn't going to take time off work to come and get him. He shoved his balled fists into the front pockets of his Dockers.

"Hey, have the police called you yet?" John asked.

"No. I haven't heard. Why, have they called you?" Jessie asked even though she knew the answer.

"Yeah. But, I didn't say anything much. And, I didn't tell them that you were there. But, I don't think it'll take long before someone else gives your name."

"There were a lot of kids there. Maybe they won't remember."

"Don't count on it. I hear Mandy's been giving interviews about that night."

"That blabbermouth. Anything to grab attention."

"Just watch yourself."

Jessie shrugged then looked around discreetly at the people walking slowly along the sidewalk and across the grass to get to the church. So many sad faces. She saw a lot of kids from school, but no one was really acknowledging each other.

I guess they don't know how they're supposed to act at a memorial service, either. It's not like it's something we learned in school.

Jessie whispered to John, "Gosh, I didn't know Anna was *that* popular."

John bent down and put his mouth close to Jessie's ear and

whispered, "Well, you know, her mom is the town shrink, they're probably all patients."

Jessie started to giggle then caught herself, shocked at her reaction.

*How can I be laughing and having fun? Isn't there something
that's supposed to turn off inside of me? Am I being disrespectful?
What are we all doing here? This summer was supposed to be the
best summer of our lives. Anna and I were going to get a job at the
mall's movie theater. What happened to our plans? Last week we
were planning her graduation party and now we're planning her
funeral. It's not fair!*

With a small punch to John's arm, Jessie let him know that this
wasn't the time to be making jokes.

Slowly, alongside other kids she'd gone to school with and people
she didn't know, Jessie climbed the steps to the church. She gazed up
at the open doors into the quiet darkness. Soft music she didn't recognize drifted out faintly from somewhere inside.

Jessie stepped gingerly across the threshold into the cool dim-
ness of the sanctuary. She stood in line with the rest of the mourners
and signed the guest book then filed down the aisle and found seats
for her and John a few pews back from Anna's mother.

Poking John in the ribs, Jessie caught his attention.

"Ow, what?" he whispered.

"Have you seen Mike yet?"

"No, not yet. He said he'd be here."

"I wonder what's keeping him?"

"Dunno. Now behave yourself."

"Fine." Jessie said then went back to studying the other people
around her. *Poor Mike. He didn't have anyone now. His dad always
off writing for the newspaper. Anna's dead. Maybe I could ...* Jessie
stopped herself from completing that thought. Shocked, she couldn't
imagine why she would think of pursuing Mike now.

Forcing all thoughts of stealing Anna's boyfriend even before the
funeral, Jessie watched Mrs. Marshall as she greeted each person
who stopped in front of her to offer their condolences. Jessie mar-
veled at her quiet strength.

*Anna's mom is so pretty. No, not pretty. Beautiful. She looks
tired, though. It must be hard. First losing her husband and now her
daughter. I wonder how she's doing?*

Jessie's eyes wandered around the rest of the dimly lit room. She
saw the principal of her school shaking hands with a man in a long
black robe.

He must be the preacher. Or is it minister? Or pastor?

Jessie gave a mental shrug of her shoulders.

*I dunno what it is. I barely know what those words mean, let
alone which one is for which religion. I wonder why we never went*

to church?

Before she could ponder that thought, the music stopped and the low whispering quieted as everyone looked up toward the podium with somber expectation.

Jessie watched as the man in the black robe stood behind the podium and adjust the microphone. He spoke softly but firmly, beginning his eulogy in memory of Anna, a young girl balanced on the precipice of life with so much ahead of her.

Jessie listened intently at first, but her quick mind bored easily. Her mind and eyes wandered around the softly lit room over a dark sea of black suits and hats. No one made eye contact.

She caught John's attention and mouthed, "Where is Mike?"

Chapter Eleven

Mike stared blankly up at the bedroom ceiling, counted to one hundred, and then started over. His low murmurings barely audible to anyone who might be sitting close by. No one was. No one ever was.

He closed his eyes and tried to forget that Anna was no longer alive; tried to forget that he didn't have anyone to talk to anymore.

My dad didn't even try to force me to go to her funeral last week. He keeps telling me that I need time. Time to get through this.

Mike pressed a hand to his mouth. *How am I supposed to get through this?*

He tried to forget the way Anna's hair smelled when it was warmed from the sun while they lay close to each other on the beach. Or the way she would start to smile and her eyes would begin to sparkle when he'd walk across the open mall area in school. Even before he was half way to her, he knew that she was giving him her full attention; no longer listening to the silly schoolgirl chattering of the flock of teen-age girls that seemed to always flutter around her.

Anna was supposed to be his forever. Mike threw his body forward and twisted until he was face down in the pillow. He slammed his fist against the wall, over and over, not even stopping when his knuckles, bloodied raw and bruised, pushed through the drywall, past the paint, and into the empty space between his wall and the next room.

Alone. Always left alone.

Mike's body jerked with dry heaves. Quickly, he hung his head over the side of his bed and waited for the spasms to stop. With his non-bloodied hand he fumbled for the pack of cigarettes on the nightstand. The crumpled pack held only one. A thought registered in the back of his mind that he had to get more cigarettes.

Sitting up, he pushed a flattened pillow behind his shoulders and kicked at the tangle of sheets and blankets on his bed. Mike sucked deeply on the cigarette then blew out a cloud of smoke as his head fell limply to the side. He forced his eyes to open by rubbing at them with his fingers, scraping the crusted eye fluids from the corner of his eyes with a dirty fingernail.

Mike tried to remember what day it was with little success. It didn't matter what day it was now that Anna was gone. His mind screamed for release. Anna couldn't be gone. Little else mattered while his denial forced all other thoughts from his mind.

"Mike?" a voice called from the other side of his door. "Are you all right?"

The voice was accompanied by a tentative rap on the door and then repeated its request.

"Leave me alone, Dad." Mike ordered, his voice hoarse from dry heaving and the cigarettes.

"Hey, if you want to talk. I'm here."

"Yeah. Right." Mike mumbled.

"What's that? I didn't quite hear you."

"Never mind. Just leave me alone, ok?"

"Well, if you change your mind, I'll be in my office working, ok?"

"So, what else is new?" Mike again mumbled, low enough so that he was sure his father wouldn't hear. "Yeah, ok." He said louder so that his dad would leave him alone.

Mike crushed out his cigarette, turned over, and faced the wall. He closed his eyes and pictured Anna smiling at him. Her face wet, her hair slicked back—water everywhere and then ... nothing until he heard screaming and his name being called. Images flashed in his mind. Kids running. Voices screaming. Girls crying. Sirens. Flashing lights. Strangers taking his Anna away. Anna. Gone. Anna. Never coming back. Anna. Gone.

Chapter Twelve

Janis turned on the lights in the main examining room to prepare for another day. She liked to come in early and set up the rooms herself. It made her feel as if she were in control. She flipped through the chart that noted last night's drop-offs and mentally counted the tables needed. Gun-shot and two car accidents.

Pretty routine for a Friday night.

Her thick, rubber-soled shoes squeaked across the old-fashioned tile floor as she walked across the room to switch on the radio. The gloomy silence scattered like the wind to The Backstreet Boys' latest teeny-bopper hit.

Janis cringed at the sappy lyrics and annoying beat. Tying on a paper cap over her gray streaked hair, she knew it wouldn't help drown out the tunes. It definitely wasn't her kind of music. But, it was the station the others liked to listen to, and majority ruled.

I'll take ol' George Strait singin' in my ear any day over this crap.

She caught her eye in the shiny metal reflection of the stainless steel cabinets to her right and grinned at herself. Shuffling her feet in a sort of two-step, she twirled and curtseyed to her make-believe crooner.

"Yes, sir, George. You an' me will two-step right on outa here."

Janis giggled self-consciously when she heard her raspy voice echo back.

Great, now I'm talking to myself. Keep it up, Janis, ol' girl. They'll find more ways than you can shake a stick at to get you to take that early retirement package, you keep this up.

───※※───

Slamming drawers and clattering metal instruments were the only sounds Helen could hear over the hip-hop beat of the radio blaring when she walked into her office an hour later.

Sounds like Janis is in one of her moods, again.

Helen crossed the hall and headed for her office instead of saying hello to her long-time assistant. She wasn't really in the mood to discuss her assistant's most recent ex-boyfriend this morning. The rain always made her feel a little melancholy and this morning's shower was no different.

On the way to her office, she stopped and grabbed her mail from the mailbox marked H. McDougal, M.E. As usual, it was filled with envelopes containing reports from various departments regarding her latest autopsies. She shuffled the envelopes, looking for anything that might require her to change direction. Nothing urgent so she kept on course directly to her office.

Helen balanced mail, briefcase, and umbrella as she unlocked the glass door with her name etched in dark letters—Helen R. McDougal, Chief Medical Examiner. Absently, she touched the letters as she pushed opened the door with her shoulder and headed inside. After five years as Chief Medical Examiner, it never ceased to amaze her to see her own name on her own office door.

She dropped her briefcase and umbrella onto the chair next to her desk then tossed the mail onto the large mahogany desk in the center of the room. Flipping the switch to her computer, she let it run through its start up program while she sorted through the mail.

She tossed invitations for speaking engagements, notices of hearings, and other calendar related mail into a pile for her secretary, Lori, to handle. If it weren't for Lori, she'd have tossed the whole lot into the trash and would end up getting annoying phone calls about why she wasn't at a particular function or meeting. Helen knew her organization skills were lackadaisical at best when it came to scheduling events, but she more than made up for it in her real work. She ran a tight operation and had received dozens of awards for excellence in her field. At that thought, her eyes wandered to the wall where Lori insisted she display every one of the awards she'd received.

Helen sighed. It wasn't about the awards or the acknowledgements. To her, it was about finding the truth. She got her satisfaction from knowing that she was able to explain to a young widow that her husband didn't kill himself by slamming his car into a pole but suffered an aneurysm or a grieving father that his son died from iodine poisoning from the lobster he ate and not from drugs as was suggested. Not all truths were so satisfying, especially today. She stared down at the toxicology report from the Marshall case. She only knew Katherine Marshall professionally, but was deeply moved by her recent loss. This report wasn't going to help.

Needing quiet and privacy, she pushed her chair back and walked around her desk to shut her door. She could still her Janis banging around as she prepared the examining rooms for the morning cases. Janis was a hard worker, but noisy. One of these days she knew she was going to have to address the noise issue and let Janis know that for her to recognize her hard work, she didn't need to hear it clear down at the end of the hall.

She pulled her phone closer and dialed the District Attorney's office.

❧❧

"Mr. Beckett?"

"Yes? Can I help you?" Charles Beckett held the heavy front door open only as much as necessary. He wasn't in the mood for company and if the two men wearing suits standing on his front porch were any indication of his ability to tell the future, he was in for some bad company. All instincts told him to shut the door quickly and firmly. But, he didn't. He stood and waited for them to go through their routine.

One of the men opened his wallet to show a badge and license. The other man stood and waited. "I'm Detective Murphy, this is Assistant State District Attorney Sam Louden. We'd like to ask your son a few questions."

"About what?" Charles made eye contact with Louden. He knew the man with the boyish looks all too well. He'd spent enough time in press conferences to know which Assistant DA's were on the fast track to political office. Louden definitely had his nose pointed toward the sky. Poking at Louden in his newspaper column had become almost a daily ritual. It wasn't like he was out to get the guy. This was an election year. His column sold a lot of newspapers.

Sam Louden answered. "Look, Beckett. This isn't a social visit."

"I didn't expect it was since you brought protection." Charles nodded toward the detective.

"Can we come in?" Louden stuck his finger in between the stiff collar of his Brooks Brothers shirt and his sweaty neck. He ran his finger around the edge of his collar hoping to remove the sweat before it stained his shirt. He looked uncomfortable.

Good, thought Charles. *He should feel uncomfortable.*

"Yeah." Charles opened the door wider and stood aside. "Come on in." He waved a hand toward the living room. "Have a seat."

"Thank you, Mr. Beckett." Detective Murphy, at least, hadn't forgotten his manners.

Louden stepped inside the cool, air-conditioned room without a word.

Charles sat in his leather recliner and pointedly asked, "Why do you want to see Mike?"

"Can we speak to your son, Mr. Beckett?"

"Look, Detective. No one speaks to Mike until they tell me what's going on, got it?"

"All right, Beckett. Keep your shirt on. This is the way it is." Louden opened his briefcase and removed a manila folder. "It's about the Marshall girl. We have the Medical Examiner's Toxicology report. There were drugs found in her system." He stared at Beckett.

Charles sat quietly without flinching beneath Louden's stare. He knew that Louden was playing him, waiting for him to make the first move. He'd wait. While he waited, he took his time lighting a cigarette from the pack on the coffee table.

The noise from the street filtered through the closed windows. Children playing. Dogs barking. The occasional car passing by. Every day noises for a warm summer day.

Detective Murphy shifted.

Louden lost his patience. "Damn it, Beckett. We got a dead girl, drugs, and your son was the last person to be seen with her. Give us a break and let us just talk to the kid."

"Are you here to arrest him?" Beckett nodded to Detective Murphy. "Why the cops?"

"Mr. Beckett," Detective Murphy interceded before the air got any thicker between the two adversaries. "This is an official investigation. I'm here to do my job."

Beckett knew he couldn't stall them for much longer. His mind raced for possible loopholes. If he refused to let them talk to Mike, they'd just come back with a court order. If it looked like they weren't cooperating with the investigation, then the police will think they have something to hide. He'd written enough columns about supposedly innocent victims hiding behind defense attorneys and refusing to talk to the police. How many times had he predicted in one of his columns that people who acted like that had something to hide, and it usually was the truth?

"All right, Louden." Beckett stabbed out the cigarette into an overflowing ashtray. "I'll get Mike. Under one condition."

"What?"

"That I control the questioning. If I feel that you're going too far or if I think Mike needs a lawyer, I call it quits and you two go away like good boys, okay?"

Louden bristled at Beckett's patronizing attitude. "Why, you sorry son-of-a—"

"We'll take it." Detective Murphy hurried to answer before Louden caused any more animosity.

"I'll get Mike." Beckett walked up the stairs toward the bedrooms.

"Do you think the kid gave this Marshall girl the drugs?" Louden asked the detective as they sat and waited.

"Probably. Who knows. From the statements given by the kids who were there, a lot of drugs and alcohol changed hands that night." Detective Murphy patted his front breast pocket in search of his cigarettes, then decided against lighting up without asking, even though he'd seen Beckett light up earlier. "Says here in the report that they found GHB in the girl's system."

"Shit." Louden said with disgust. "That's all we need is a date rape gone bad."

"Those kids ain't been too keen on talking."

"Who's working the kids?"

"Robles. He's good. He's worked them kids and gotten a lot more out of them than anyone else could."

"Yeah, I've heard that. He's got a way with them. He's the one who gave you the lead to this kid?"

Pulling the papers closer, Detective Murphy glanced through them quickly. "The Beckett kid is ... was this girl's boyfriend. Seems they had an argument earlier witnessed by a few kids at the party. But, from what we can gather, they made up and were staying close to each other for the rest of the night. Report says that Mike Beckett wasn't with her when she was found."

"Who found her?"

"That we're still working on. Seems we have conflicting stories."

"Why?"

"One kid says he's the one who found her, while other kids say that there was a girl who found her. We're still following up on that."

"Good, find that girl. We'll need her ..." Louden stopped speaking as Mike and his father entered the room.

Great. Another stoner. Louden thought to himself as he took in Mike's dirty hair sticking up in several places about his head and clothes that looked as if he'd slept in them for the last week.

"Mike, this is Detective Murphy and Assistant District Attorney Louden. They want to ask you a few questions about Anna's drowning." Beckett kept his eye on Louden as he made the introductions.

Louden extended a hand. "Hello, Mike. Nice to meet you." After shaking Mike's dirty hand, Louden surreptitiously wiped his own on the side of his trousers while Mike shook hands with Detective Murphy.

Mike slumped into an overstuffed chair then made a grab for the cigarettes on the table. Without asking permission, he lit one up, then blew the cloudy smoke in the direction of Louden. "Yeah? So."

Waving a hand to dissipate the smoke, Louden asked, "Mike, can you tell me what happened at the sce—I mean, party?" He didn't need to look at Beckett to know he was staring a hole into him.

"I dunno."

"What do you mean, you don't know? You were there weren't you?"

"Yeah, I guess so."

"Mike," Detective Murphy interrupted. "We understand that Anna Marshall was your girlfriend."

"So." Mike slumped lower into the chair and stared off into space.

"Could you tell us about your relationship with Anna."

"We hung out together."

"Wasn't your relationship with Anna more than just 'hanging out'?" Detective Murphy opened his notebook and reviewed his notes. "According to students from your high school, you two were practically inseparable. Were you engaged?"

"Engaged? Please. I'd know if my son was engaged." Charles Beckett gave his son a questioning look.

Mike said nothing.

Sam Louden wasn't interested in whether Mike and Anna were engaged. He wanted to know about the drugs and alcohol. "Mike, were you drinking at the party?"

"Drinking? I dunno. Probably. There was a lot of soda and stuff there."

"I'm not talking about soda. What about alcohol? Was there alcohol at the party? Were you drinking any alcohol?"

"Probably."

"Probably there was alcohol or probably you were drinking alcohol?" Sam Louden's impatience was beginning to wane.

Mike shot a questioning look to his father. Charles shook his head. Mike spoke like a monotone parrot, "I can't answer that question on the grounds I might incriminate myself."

"Like father like son."

"Oh, come now, Louden. You don't expect the boy to admit to drinking when he's underage, do you?" Charles Beckett asked.

"All right, Beckett. We'll do it your way ... for now." Louden took his time rummaging through the file folder. "Mike, what about drugs. Were you aware of drug use going on at the party?"

"Whadda mean?" Mike shifted slightly in the chair and crossed one foot over the other.

"Drugs. Pot. Marijuana. Cocaine. Ecstasy. GHB. Crack. I'm sure it's not the first time you've heard these terms."

Detective Murphy tried to smooth the tense situation. "There's no reason why we need any animosity. Mike, we're not implying you were taking drugs or drinking alcohol. What we need to know is if you saw anyone, and if so, who. Anna had drugs and alcohol in her system when she drowned and we'd like to know how they got there."

"I dunno. I wasn't with her every second of the night."

"Well, you just don't seem to be very cooperative today, do you, Mike?" Louden shuffled the papers back into the file folder.

Mike shrugged his shoulders.

"I tell you what. Maybe your memory will come back to you if we bring you down to the police station to answer some questions."

"Whoa, fellas. Are you arresting my son?"

"Not right now, we're not; but, we'll be in touch." Louden stood. "Let's go, Detective Murphy. We're not going get anywhere asking questions today. We'll put together a formal request for Mr. Beckett's presence downtown."

"You do that." Charles stood as well and walked to the door to show the assistant DA and the detective out.

"Have a good day, Mr. Beckett." Detective Murphy said as he walked out.

"You won't be talking to my kid again without a lawyer present, got it, Louden?"

"I *got* it, Beckett. And, if you want to make things easier on your kid, you might want to encourage him to tell us what he knows."

Outside in the bright sunshine, thunder rumbled in the distance. Detective Murphy scanned the skies for dark clouds indicating the afternoon summer storms. "Looks like rain. We could use it." He kicked at a brown patch of grass. "These water restrictions are tough on everybody."

Louden nodded his head absently. "Hey, Murph. Can you drop me off at my car?"

"Yeah, sure, no problem. You thinking of heading over to the Marshall place?"

Louden opened the car door and slid into the hot car. "Yeah, how'd you know?"

Detective Murphy laughed as he slid behind the steering wheel and started the car. "I'm not a detective for nothing, sir."

"Smartass. Just take me to my car."

"Yes, sir."

Chapter Thirteen

Katherine opened her front door to find Sam Louden on her doorstep. "Mr. Louden, I wasn't expecting you." She smoothed a nervous hand down her black silk blouse and made sure the ends were tucked into her slim black skirt.

"Am I interrupting, Mrs. Marshall?"

"No. No, please come in." She stood aside to let the assistant DA into her home.

Sam stepped inside and surveyed the quiet elegance. He stepped onto the tiled foyer and waited for Mrs. Marshall to close the door.

"Please, won't you come into the living room and have a seat?"

"Thank you."

"Can I offer you something to drink? Iced tea, perhaps?"

"Yes, thank you, if it's no bother."

Katherine headed for the kitchen after showing Sam Louden to a comfortable wing-backed chair next to the fireplace. "No, it's no bother. I kind of like having something to do."

Katherine busied herself in her pale blue tiled kitchen. She filled two tall glasses with crushed ice from the refrigerator's dispenser. She poured sun-brewed tea from a large container into a glass pitcher. Adding a plate of sliced lemon and a small sugar bowl to the tray, she looked about the kitchen to see if she had forgotten anything. Spying the iced teaspoons she snatched them up along with a few napkins then carried the tray into the living room.

"Don't get up." She said as Sam Louden stood as she entered the room.

"Mrs. Marshall, let me help you with that." Louden took the tray and sat it on the polished and immaculate coffee table. He noted the stark contrast to the Beckett's messier home. "And, call me Sam, please."

"All right. Sam. And you can call me Katherine." She sat on the sofa and poured the tea then offered lemon and sugar.

"Mrs. Marshall, I mean ... Katherine." He modified his approach when Katherine frowned.

"I hope you feel up to a few questions."

"I guess so. What can I help you with?" Katherine took a long sip of the cool tangy amber liquid.

"I'd like to ask you about Anna's relationship with Michael Beckett."

"Mike? They were friends."

"Do you have any idea how ... close they were?" Sam shifted in the chair and took a drink of his tea.

"Well, they did see a lot of each other. What else do you want to know?"

"Were they dating exclusively?"

"I'm not sure if *dating* is the correct term, these days, Sam." Katherine sat back and crossed one nylon-clad knee over the other. "Do you have any children, Sam?"

"No. I'm not married."

"Oh."

"I'm divorced. My ex-wife and I never got around to having children before we decided to call it quits." He wiped his hands with a napkin. "Just as well."

"Teenagers nowadays don't really date. They mostly hang out in a crowd. Anna and Mike were part of the same crowd."

"Katherine, if I could be frank, did you know if Anna was sexually active?"

"What?" Katherine's hand shook. She quickly put her glass down, but not before a few drops of her tea spilled onto her skirt. She dabbed at the wet spot. She knew the tea couldn't be seen on her black skirt, but she didn't want it to ruin the silk. She excused herself to add a little cold water to the spot.

While he waited, Sam's eyes wandered around the elegantly decorated, yet understated room. The color scheme matched perfectly from the beige carpet to the moss green throw pillows that matched the leaves in the flower-patterned upholstery on the sofa. The mantle over the fireplace held crystal candlestick holders and candles the same color as the throw pillows.

I wonder if she paid as much attention to her own daughter as she did in getting all the details right in this room? Sam turned in his chair to look around the rest of the room.

He noticed a lack of knick-knacks strewn about the room like at his sister's house. Instead, he noticed a well-placed vase on a sofa table filled with fresh-cut flowers. He admired Katherine's decorating adeptness.

"What are you smiling at, Mr. Louden?"

Sam shuffled to his feet quickly. "I'm sorry. I was just admiring your room. I thought we agreed on 'Sam'?"

"Thank you." Katherine said as she continued to stand. "I'm not sure this is the right time to ... Mr. Louden, I think you should go."

"Your right, Mrs. Marshall. I'm sorry for mentioning it. However, there are a few things we need to clear up. And, I'd like your help, if possible."

"Mr. Louden—"

"Sam." Louden said with a quiet, reverent tone. "Please."

"Won't you please sit down, then?"

"I will if you will." Sam half-chuckled at this attempt to lighten the mood. He pulled a file folder from his briefcase and handed a copy of the medical examiner's report to Katherine as she took her place on the sofa. "Here are the results of the tests done by the medical examiner."

Katherine took the report and skimmed its contents.

"As you can see, the medical examiner found alcohol in Anna's system."

"What is this methylene-diox ..." Katherine stumbled over the pronunciation.

"Ah, yeah. Methylene-dioxy-methamphetamine; MDMA for short. To the kids, it's Ecstasy."

"Ecstasy? The date rape drug?" Katherine's faced registered shock.

"Well, it's been used by men to get women to *relax* and lose their inhibitions so they can have sex with them. But, we've found that teenagers in dance clubs use it to get a more euphoric *high*."

"Dance clubs? Anna never went to any dance clubs. There isn't even any around here."

"Dance clubs, or raves as the teenagers call them, aren't real clubs, in the sense that there is a tax paying owner who filed the proper licenses. They're usually found in an old warehouse, or a barn, or even disguised as teen clubs. These clubs are popping up all over. As soon as we find one and close it down, another opens. They're places where teenagers can pay a cover price at the door and dance. Unfortunately, more often than not, drugs like Ecstasy are sold as well as alcohol."

"But, that makes these clubs illegal, doesn't it?" Katherine absently folded and unfolded the report while she listened to Sam.

"Yes, but that's not stopping someone from making a buck."

"What does this Ecstasy do? Is it dangerous?"

"To some kids with health problems it can be lethal. It's a mood enhancer, basically. Kids take it because it makes the music sound better or makes them dance better. It gives them a mood boost. Everybody loves everybody, you know?"

"You mean, like an anti-depressant?"

"Basically, yes." Sam remembered Katherine's profession. "I'm sure, as a psychiatrist you've run across patients who needed drug treatments?"

Katherine's lips curved upward into a small smile. She'd gotten this a lot from those who misunderstood her profession. "I'm a cognitive behavioral therapist." She continued as she watched Sam's face stay blank, "a psychologist, not a psychiatrist. And, we try not to pre-scribe drugs in our treatment. We prefer to help the client change their behavior and surroundings instead of depending on drugs to do it for them."

"Oh. Well, I kind of thought that it was all the same."

"That's okay. Most people do. Mental health doesn't always mean drugs and psychiatric treatments."

"Katherine, about your daughter. The report contains facts. The fact is she had drugs and alcohol in her system at the time of her death. Now, I'd like to think that she was a good girl." He held up his hand as he spoke to stop Katherine from interrupting. "I'm sure that basically, she was. And, if so, then someone gave her those drugs. I'd like to find out who it was. As you can see, the medical examiner cited the cause of death as inconclusive."

"What does that mean?"

"I spoke to the medical examiner when she called with the test results. It means that your daughter had enough of the drug in her system that she could have been relaxed to the point of drowning. Now, that says to me that someone is responsible for your daughter's death, possibly, the person who gave her the drugs. I'd like to see that person held responsible, wouldn't you?"

"Of course. Yes." Katherine's mind raced to absorb this new in-formation.

"Sam, was this drug, umm ... I mean, was my daughter addicted?" Katherine stammered as she asked the question, not quite meeting the assistant D.A.'s eyes.

"From what we know about Ecstasy, it's not habit forming."

Sam reached out a hand to gently touch Katherine's shaking one. "I don't think your daughter was an addict," he said.

"All of this is news to me, you know?"

"I know. Unfortunately, I've seen it before."

"What?"

"Having to give a person news about a loved one's private activi-ties. Activities that they might not have a clue about." Sam swallowed the last of his iced tea. He grimaced a bit at the watered down taste. The ice had long melted. "For instance, your daughter's ... uh ... activi-ties."

"Oh." Katherine sat in silence, a pensive look on her face. "You're talking about sex, aren't you?"

"Yes. Katherine, the medical examiner does a very thorough ex-amination of the ..." he coughed into his hand then continued, "the body when it's brought in for an autopsy." He tried to cover his embar-rassment by pulling out a copy of the report to read from. "Your daugh-ter showed signs of recent sexual contact. The medical examiner col-lected semen from her ..." he coughed again, "her vagina." He contin-ued speaking quickly. "We are only assuming that it was the Beckett kid, since the two of them seemed to be an item. We'll know for sure when the DNA tests are done to confirm a match."

Katherine stared at him with a pair of vacant eyes. "You mean ... Anna was having sex?" She shook her head. "No. That can't be right." She stood and crossed the room.

Sam watched as the slender woman wrapped her arms about her body as she paced. After years of giving this kind of news to people, he knew that she needed some time. He also knew that the first reaction was always denial. He felt sorry for her. She seemed so lost; so alone in this perfect room.

"Katherine. The medical examiner doesn't make mistakes. It's her job to be completely thorough."

"But, Anna would have said something. We'd always been so open with each other. We talked about sex and stuff. We talked about birth control. She promised me that when she was ready she'd come to me and we'd get her on the pill."

Sam shuffled the papers back into his briefcase. He knew from experience that this bit of news was going to take time to sink in. His best bet was to get the Beckett kid downtown and have him give a blood sample. He needed to contact Sgt. Robles to follow up on locating the girl from the party. "Katherine, I think I should go."

Katherine stopped her pacing. "Sam."

"Hmm?"

"Anna was a good girl." Katherine reached out and touched the sleeve of his jacket. "My daughter didn't take drugs and she wasn't promiscuous. Find out who did this."

Sam looked down into her pleading eyes. She hadn't had much sleep. Close up, he could see dark patches around her eyes. There was tautness about her face. He covered her small hand with his larger one and squeezed it carefully. "I will."

"Sam?"

"Yes?"

"Make them pay."

Sam nodded without speaking. That reaction too, was typical of the survivors. They always wanted someone to be held accountable for taking their loved ones from them. In this case, he'd be only too happy to find whoever was responsible for cutting short such a young life.

Just as he was about to step through the open doorway, he stopped. "Oh, by the way. We're getting some conflicting reports that there was a girl who found Anna in the pool. Conveniently, the other teenagers are having trouble remembering her name. Maybe you can help?"

"I can try. Do you have a description?"

"Small girl. Short hair. Real firecracker. Did Anna know anyone that fit that description?"

"Jessie."

"Jessie?"

"Anna's best friend. Jessie Slater." Katherine swallowed hard. "They had connived to stay out that night. Anna told me she was spending the night at Jessie's house, and apparently, Jessie told her mother that she was spending the night here."

"Would you happen to have her telephone number?"

"Yes. Let me get it for you. I'll be right back."

Katherine shut the door after the assistant district attorney left. Automatically, she cleaned up the iced tea glasses and put away the sugar and lemon slices.

It wasn't fair, she thought. Hadn't she been a good mother? Didn't her daughter do well in school and have nice clothes and a beautiful house? Hadn't she suffered enough when her husband died? Katherine stood at the sliding glass doors to her lanai. She watched the wind bend the small palm tree in her back yard. The blooms on the crape myrtle rustled. Noticing the dark clouds overhead, she hurried outside to pull in patio chairs that were strewn about the pool deck. *How many times have I told Anna to put the chairs away when she was finished?* Katherine cried out at the harsh thought that had crossed her mind. She crumbled into one of the plastic chairs and put her head into her hands. Never again would Anna have friends over to laze about the pool. Never again would she have to remind Anna to clean up the lanai after her friends left. Katherine sobbed in her hands.

It just wasn't fair!

She beat her fist against her knees. Anna had so much to live for. She excelled in school. She was going to college in the fall. They'd made so many plans for her future. Katherine let the tears fall. She cried for her daughter. She cried for herself. She cried for her unborn grandchildren and she cried for a man who never got to see his daughter graduate from high school. Most of all, she cried out at the injustice of life. The logical, clinical part of her knew that she needed to talk to someone about this, but the more selfish part of her wanted to wallow in her self-pity.

So caught up in her thoughts, she didn't notice the flash of lightning as it streaked across the sky. But, the resonating boom of thunder caused her to jump and cast a fretful glance at the threatening sky toiling with dark clouds.

She finished putting the chairs away then rushed inside for cover. Already, large drops of rain spattered the concrete around the pool. Soon, the clouds would open up and the afternoon storms would temporarily drench the parched ground.

Without bothering with cooking herself dinner, Katherine ate a small salad and then prepared for bed.

Huddled under the designer sheets of pale apricot and matching comforter only a slight shade darker, Katherine listened to the soft music playing from her bedside stereo. She barely noticed the raging storm outside as she thought about how she raised Anna. Should she have been stricter with her? Would it have made a difference? She hadn't found it necessary to question every movement her daughter made. Should she have called Jessie's parents to verify that Anna was there? Did that make her a bad parent for trusting her daughter? Was she just as guilty of her daughter's death for letting her daughter run around with a crowd that drank and did drugs even when she didn't know?

Katherine pondered the possibility that she may not have been as close to her daughter as she imagined. She couldn't remember the last time they had a heart to heart talk. Anna had been so busy with school and other activities the last couple of years; especially this last year, her senior year. Katherine recalled the many occasions that she and her daughter would pass each other while one or the other was coming or going. Anna had honors classes, the school newspaper, choir practice, and even drama practice. Katherine sighed, her heart heavy.

Could she have said something differently? Should she have been more prying? What was her life to be like without Anna?

Katherine fell into an exhausted sleep while she tried to sort through the endless possibilities.

Katherine woke late after a fitful night of sleep. The sun had already burned off the morning fog. She rubbed her temples, already feeling the beginning of a headache. Sluggish and lethargic, she pulled herself out of bed to tend to her bathroom functions. Shuffling her feet across the cool bathroom tile and back into the bedroom, she heaved a dejected sigh at the unmade bed. Deciding against making it, she chose instead to climb back in.

Curling into a fetal position, Katherine hugged a pillow to her chest.

Chapter Fourteen

Katherine cuddled her pillow remembering other times when she'd lay in her bed, cuddling her favorite doll. She'd cover her head with a pillow while her mother and father fought.

Luckily, those times weren't often because her father wasn't home much. He worked as a railroad conductor and his assignments took him from home most weeks. They all coped in their own way while daddy was gone. Margaret spent a lot of time at school and with her boyfriend. Katherine was too young for boys to be a distraction for her. She usually ended up cleaning up after her mother.

Katherine couldn't remember when she discovered that her mother's drinking was a problem. Maybe she always knew it deep down. She drank most when daddy was gone. But, as time went by, she'd drink when daddy was home too. When daddy stopped coming home she drank all the time. Katherine never understood until she graduated from high school what had happened to her father. Margaret tried to explain that it was a heart attack brought on by the stress of his job and poor circulation. Katherine knew different. Daddy died of a broken heart.

Katherine bore the brunt of her mother's anger. Margaret stayed out of her mother's way and ended up marrying as soon as she graduated from high school. Katherine remembered the rush of anger and envy that encompassed her as she watched her sister leave with her new husband. Her mother latched onto Katherine and kept a tight rein on her life.

Katherine had no life outside of her home. She wasn't allowed to date or socialize with the other kids in her neighborhood or school. All the household chores fell onto Katherine's small shoulders. Her mother's few lucid moments became Katherine's opportunity to …

Katherine sat up in bed. Was that it? Did she try to raise Anna in a more lenient way, over compensating for her own strict upbringing? Was that just as bad as being raised strict?

Had she contributed to her daughter's death?

Chapter Fifteen

"They've arrested Anna's boyfriend?"

"Yes, I got the call from the assistant district attorney this morning." Katherine shuffled papers on her desk as she spoke to her administrative assistant, Jennie.

"Isn't Mike Beckett the son of Charles Beckett that newspaper columnist?"

"Yes. Although, I've never really met him. Mike and Anna dated, but we never socialized as a family. I saw him and said hello at graduation."

"I hear he's a hot head." Jennie spun around in her chair. "Have you read any of his stuff?"

"Not on a regular basis. Some of the headlines catch my eye as I read the paper. He targets political figures a lot, doesn't he?"

"Yeah. His targets have included judges, attorneys, community leaders; basically anyone who gives him something to write about. I'm sure he won't be leaving this incident alone."

"What incident? His son's arrest? Wouldn't he want to lay low when it comes to personal issues?"

"Not if he can turn it around. I hear he's been prone to use his column to sway public opinion."

Katherine raised her eyebrows in Jennie's direction. "You hear quite a bit, don't you?"

"Yeah, well don't say I didn't warn you."

Katherine responded with a small smile. Jennie felt sorry for her. "Katherine, you should take some time off."

"I have too much work to do."

"Your patients can wait. You need to take care of yourself first."

"Thanks for thinking of me, Jen. But, I have an obligation to take care of my patients. They didn't ask for my help only when I feel like it. They need me."

Jennie sighed. "Katherine, at least refer the newer patients to Dr. Jeffries. He does it to you enough times."

"Well, you might be right." Katherine turned and glanced about the room. "I don't know. I just don't like letting others do my work.

Maybe we can just try juggling my schedule some more." She straightened her blouse. "Besides, it's either stay alone at home, or come here and work and keep myself busy. I'd rather keep busy."

"Your sister isn't staying with you anymore?"

"No, how could she? She has her own family to take care of. Especially since my niece just had another baby."

Jennie hid the pity on her face. Then she turned back, remembering the start of their conversation. "So, are the police saying the drowning wasn't an accident?"

"I don't think that's what it means. Apparently, there were drugs and alcohol at the party and they're accusing Mike of giving drugs to Anna."

"Drugs? Alcohol? Our little Anna? Oh, God, Katherine, there must be some mistake."

"That's what I thought at first too. But, I called the medical examiner and confirmed the report." Katherine leapt from her chair and paced the small outer office where her patients waited until they were escorted into her quiet sanctum. "I still can't believe it. I've been wandering around in a fog since I found out."

She gave only a cursory glance at the two sofas decorated in muted tones that faced each other. Small throw pillows invited anyone who enters to settle in and be comfortable. She disliked the stiff hardback chairs that usually appeared in waiting rooms. She wanted her patients to feel comfortable and at home. Seeking counseling could be stressful. She wanted to put forth an image of comfort and caring that surrounded the patient as soon as they walked through her door.

"Jennie, did I ever thank you for rescheduling my patients?"

"Yes, you did. At least ten times, by the way."

Katherine nodded and forced a smile. "Did I ever tell you I'd be lost without you?"

"I'll remind you that you said that when it comes to my yearly review."

Katherine laughed despite her melancholy. Jennie had been with her from the first day she opened up her practice. Jennie had won her over with her efficiency at keeping up with her dictation, handling insurance billing processes, and providing just the right touch of friendliness to keep the patients at ease.

The telephone interrupted their chat and Jennie went back to work juggling Katherine's schedule.

≈≈

"Mike, do you understand what's happening here?"

"Yeah."

"Hey! Look at me, kid. This isn't just going to go away when you wake up tomorrow morning. We're talking serious stuff here." Assistant District Attorney Louden slammed his hand on the desk separating him and Mike.

"What?" Mike cast bored, drowsy eyes to the man sitting next to him. "Can he do this to me?"

"He's trying to explain to you about the charges filed against you by his office, Mike." Frank Peters put his elbows on the table and leaned forward.

"Yeah I know. I heard him."

"Do you understand what he's telling you?"

"Yeah. He's saying I killed Anna." Mike thrust out his lower lip and tucked his chin into his chest. "But, I didn't do it."

"Louden, let me sp—"

The door slammed open with a loud crash. "What's going on here?" Charles Beckett went to his son's side of the table and awkwardly placed a hand on Mike's shoulder.

Mike shrugged his dad's hand off. "Dad ..."

Frank Peters spoke up. "It's okay Charlie. We didn't go into any details and I wouldn't let Louden question Mike without you."

"Good." Charles turned to Louden. "So, what kind of trumped up charge do we have here?"

"Dump the animosity, Beckett. Your son is being charged with third-degree murder. We will prove that he knowingly gave Anna Marshall an overdose of the drug, Ecstasy."

Beckett turned to the lawyer he'd kept on retainer ever since his column went syndicated. "Is he for real?" He used his thumb to point at the assistant district attorney.

"Yeah, unfortunately he is. The state of Florida recently passed some legislature that cracks down really hard on underage deaths related to alcohol or drugs. This case has both according to the medical examiner's report." He shoved a copy of the report to Mike's dad.

Beckett ignored the report and turned to the assistant district attorney. "So, some girl drowns. It's an election year, so you're going to make a federal case out of it?"

"Watch it, Beckett." Louden struggled to keep his anger under control. It wouldn't help if he lost his temper and ended up as the subject of Beckett's column tomorrow.

"Do you honestly think you can prove that Mike was the one who gave the girl drugs? Don't you think she could have gotten them on her own?"

"That's what we're going to prove." Louden shoved a file folder back into his briefcase. "We'll see you at the arraignment tomorrow. I don't foresee any problems in getting the judge to set a quick trial date."

"We'll see about that. I've already prepared a motion for dismissal." Frank Peters handed Louden a copy of the brief.

"Waste of paper, Peters." Louden put the brief in his briefcase along with his other files. He turned without another word and left the room.

"How long do I have to stay in jail?"

"Frank? Have you covered the bail yet?"

"That's next. The arraignment is this afternoon. We'd better get over to the courtroom." Peters rapped on the door and motioned for the guard to come in.

Mike slid further into his seat, insolence shown over his face. "Can't I stay here?"

Beckett threw a questioning look at Peters then to the guard.

Peters shook his head silently.

"I'm sorry, son." Beckett patted Mike on the shoulder. "It won't be much longer now."

The guard pulled out a pair of handcuffs and motioned for Mike to stand. Mike stood after a moment of silence then held out his hands, wrists together.

"Oh, come on. Are those really necessary?" Beckett turned to Frank.

"Sir, it's policy." The guard spoke for the first time. "Let's go, Mike." He placed a hand at Mike's back and propelled him toward the door.

Frank called out to Mike, "We'll see you in the courtroom later this afternoon. Hang in their, kid."

"Hey, dad?"

"Yeah?"

"Can I have some cigarettes?"

Beckett pulled out a pack from his pocket and handed it to Mike. "Here, this should last you until this afternoon."

Mike fumbled with the pack with his cuffed hands. "Some help?"

Before Beckett could help his son, the guard plucked the pack of cigarettes from the boy's hands and shoved them into the front pocket of Mike's t-shirt. "Time to go."

"Shit!" Charles Beckett slammed a fist against the wall after his son was escorted from the interview room. "How can this be happening? Two weeks ago the only thing we're thinking about is Mike graduating from high school. Now, he's being charged with murder? What is wrong with this fucking world?"

"Stay calm, Charlie."

"How can I stay calm? My son is stuck in jail. My entire life is turned upside down." Beckett scratched at his head with nervous hands. "I need to do something. I can't wait for action."

"We're doing what needs to be done, Charlie. This takes time. The process takes time. I'll request a fast-track if it gets to that point."

"Fast track?"

"Yeah, we need to play on the sympathy of the community. It's a horrible tragedy that the Marshall girl died, but to ruin a young boy's life? To make him pay for her actions? No. That won't happen if we can get the community involved."

"Are you saying what I think you're saying, Frank?"

Frank turned to his friend. "Just don't be too obvious, okay?"

∽≈

"Hey, Mike what was it like being in jail?"

"Dude, it wasn't as cool as it looks on TV." Mike sucked deep of the joint being passed around. "But, I was in a cell with this one guy." Mike snorted and coughed as he guzzled a beer. "He was such a jerk. He kept telling me he could get me hooked up with some guys if I needed anything."

"No kidding?" Jeff pulled open a bag of corn chips and crunched loudly.

"Yeah, get this. The guy he was going to hook me up with? Paul!"

"No way!" Wet corn chip crumbs flew from Jeff's mouth.

"Yeah, wait'll I tell Paul."

"Oh, hey, I heard Paul was questioned by the police about you." Robbie muttered between swigs of his beer.

"Where'd you hear that?" Jeff asked.

"He told Dave. Dave told Mark. Mark told my cousin Stephano. Stephano told me."

"Get off it, Robbie." Mike threw his empty beer can in Robbie's general direction.

Robbie ducked. "I'm being serious. We all got questioned by the cops." He flung his arms out toward the rest of the group. "Ain't that right?"

Heads nodded.

"Whatcha been telling the cops?" Mike asked.

"Not much to tell them. We all were there when Jessie found Anna. It was an accident."

"What about you, Mike? What kinda questions have they asked you?"

"Like, where'd I get the drugs. Where'd I get the alcohol."

"You finger Paul?"

"Fuck no! You know the code!"

"Chill out, dude. We know the code. We all took the oath."

"Yeah, well remember it next time you're asked who got stuff for the party. Got it?"

"Yeah, I got it."

"And, don't forget we all are covering for each other, right?"

"Shit, Mike. You act like we killed Anna. It was an accident, right?"

Mike drew a deep breath. "Right." He ignored the rest of the guys lounging around the room. Anna's face floated past his eyes. "I gotta split."

"Yo, Mike. Wait up. I need a ride."

"No can do, Robbie. Get a ride from somebody else. I got stuff to do." Mike checked his pocket for car keys then headed for the door. He disregarded the calls and comments from his friends as he slammed his way out of the house, jumped into his car, and sped away.

ℳ ℳ

Jessie couldn't believe her luck. She'd been wandering through the mall without much to do when she saw Mike.

"Hey, Mike." Jessie called as she caught up with him in front of the pretzel store.

"Hi, Jess."

"How's it going?" Jessie asked as she gave him a warm hug.

"Fine."

"You don't look fine. You look like crap."

"Gee. Thanks."

"You know what I mean." Jessie pulled his arm and propelled him to a small table with two chairs. "Let's sit."

Mike allowed himself to be led through the shopping crowd and sat across from Jessie. "I guess you heard, huh?"

"Yeah, I did. I think it sucks. How can they think you'd do anything to hurt Anna? God, you guys loved each other."

"I know." Mike traced the zig-zag pattern on the table with a grimy fingernail.

"Mike?" Jessie covered his hand with hers. "Is there anything I can do?"

Mike shrugged.

"I mean it, Mike. I don't want to see anything happen to you. I ... well, you know, I care about you."

Mike turned his palm up and held Jessie's hand. "Thanks, Jess. I've always liked you too."

"Yeah?" Jessie straightened a bit, almost blushing. "I didn't know. I mean, I always wished ..."

Mike held her hand tighter; squeezing her fingers. "Jessie, I can't go back to jail. I just can't."

"Tell me what you need me to do."

Chapter Sixteen

"That boy has suffered enough."

"I just can't believe that he's on trial for that girl's death."

Nick sat with his back to the group of gossiping women in the booth adjacent to his. He sat up straight when he heard the next woman speak.

"Well, I just don't understand why that woman has to put that poor boy through this. Can't she stop it?"

"Who knows what's going on with her? Katherine Marshall is one cool cucumber if you ask me."

Nick made a face at the wall. *No one asked, you old biddy.*

"Can I get you anything else, sir?" the tired waitress asked.

"No, thank you. I'll just finish up with my coffee and then that'll be it. Could you bring the check?"

"Sure thing, hon." The waitress picked up Nick's plate. "Take your time."

Nick sipped his coffee while he eavesdropped.

"Did you read about her in the paper this week? They said that her husband died before she moved to Bridgeway. She's supposed to be some big hotshot psychologist or something."

"Hey I read that too. Jeez, first her husband then her daughter. You wonder sometimes, you know, if God doesn't take care of situations like this in His grand scheme."

"What do you mean, Evie? Like God did this to Katherine Marshall on purpose?"

"Well, maybe. I mean, think of it. She's a career woman, all wrapped up in helping other people. We read about it all the time. These women that think they can have it all, family, career, and then it all falls apart."

"These women nowadays, they spend all their time away from their families, no wonder that their kids are out running wild, drinking and doing drugs. Did you hear that the dead girl had drugs in her?"

"Drugs and drinking. Shameful. That's what it is, shameful."

"That's right. Just like that column in today's paper. Remember the one we read this morning? Beckett's Mind, wasn't it? It said that if more women stayed home and put their family first then there would be a lot less crime."

"The family life has gone the way of the do-do bird."

"Evie, you sure do have a way with words."

"Besides, I don't think that I read anywhere that Katherine Marshall was filing charges, did I? Doesn't the prosecutor have the option to file charges on behalf of the state?"

Gee, one of them has a clue, Nick thought with a touch of sarcasm.

Laughter burst from behind Nick. "Where'd you hear that, Sadie? Last night's Law & Order?"

"Oh, come on, let's get serious. Who wants dessert?"

Nick drained his cup and tossed a few bills onto the table as the women tittered at their little joke. He'd had enough.

Clenching his fists, he stomped past the womens' booth and out of the restaurant. He'd read the same column this morning over breakfast. He figured the best way to express his opinion of what Beckett wrote was to use the paper to wrap up the banana peel from his breakfast.

Mrs. Marshall doesn't seem to be catching any breaks. He hadn't talked to her since he carried her into her house, but he'd waved in passing the last few times he'd been by to take care of her lawn.

He'd followed the trial in the newspaper along with the rest of the city. He shuddered to even think how he'd react if he were in a similar situation.

❦

Katherine sat stone-faced and unblinking behind the prosecutor's table. She'd listened to Sam Louden rationalize the reasons for accusing Anna's boyfriend for her death. She'd kept quiet while the defense attorney for Mike Beckett painted a different picture of her daughter. One that portrayed Anna as a party girl, loose and fast. Sam had prepared her for the defense, but it still hurt to think what they were saying about her daughter.

The last straw was listening to those teenagers Anna had called her friends support the defense's theory that she had been into drugs and drinking.

"Sam!" Katherine called the assistant district attorney's name through the crowds of reporters, photographers, and onlookers.

"Katherine, can we talk while we walk? I have to check in with my office before we go back."

"Why are you letting them talk about Anna like that?" Katherine's voice rose and grew more agitated with each step. "Why don't you object? Can't you do something?"

"Katherine, the defense attorney is well within his legal bounds to use Anna's alleged reputation."

"Reputation? Reputation! Anna doesn't have a reputation."

"Try not to let it upset you so much. They have the right to do this."

"They have the right? What about Anna's rights? Doesn't she count?"

"Look Katherine, I'm not representing Anna, or you. I'm representing the state of Florida."

"Well, let me tell them about Anna, then. Let me refute their attacks."

"You'll be called as a witness. But, before you are, we'll go over our questions and the questions I expect the defense to ask you. Keep your cool, Katherine. Don't let them shake you."

"I'm furious, Sam. Furious."

"I know. Just keep it under control when it's your turn on the stand."

"I'm not sure if I can listen to much more of this."

"Just another day or so. Then it'll be over."

"Over for who? None of this will bring Anna back, Sam. My life will never be the same again. Never!" Katherine veered right and rushed into the ladies' room. She didn't care if she left without saying goodbye. Sam Louden would just have to understand.

She slammed the stall door and turned the lock. She searched in vain for tissues in her purse. Frustrated, Katherine tore several sheets from the toilet paper roll and dabbed at her eyes. She adjusted her suit jacket and straightened her skirt. She put her hand on the lock. Voices entering the ladies' room stopped her from opening the stall door. She wasn't quite ready to face anyone yet.

She stood in the tiny space waiting for the women to leave before she ventured out. Their conversation startled her.

"I can't believe this case even made it to trial."

"I bet it was that Marshall woman's dealing."

"Katherine Marshall? The dead girl's mother?"

"Yeah, her. You seen her in court, right?"

"Yeah. She just sits there. No emotion on her face at all. Like she could be sitting anywhere."

"I bet she's got some grudge against Beckett or Beckett's kid."

"Did you read today's paper?"

"Mmm hhhmmmm."

"Did you see Beckett's column this morning?"

"Yeah, I did. You know, sometimes I don't always agree with what he writes, but today's column really hit home. I mean, he writes that women who choose a career outside of the home are just asking for trouble. I know just what he means. My sister, up Georgia way, she decided to work after her boys were born. Let me tell you, those boys are hellions on wheels. Now, take me and my family. They come first. Always have. Always will."

"Yep, me too. Kevin and I decided when I first got pregnant that I'd stay home with the kids while he worked. We don't want our kids growing up without a real family environment."

Katherine waited until the voices had faded and the outer door closed. She slowly exited the stall and walked to the sink. Her ashen face stared back at her from the water-spotted mirror.

✿

"Louden, you listen to me."

"Yes, sir?" Sam sat on the corner of his desk and faced the deputy mayor of Bridgeway.

"The mayor doesn't want this trial to panic the city unnecessarily. You get your conviction, if you can on that Beckett boy, but leave out the so-called rampant drug and alcohol abuse among our fair city. That's just libel and a deliberate attempt to slander our city and its communities."

"The teenagers were drinking and they were doing drugs."

"You found drugs and alcohol in the dead girl. Did you find them in anyone else?"

"Well, no one else died, sir."

"See there. No epidemic."

Sam laughed. "Come now, you can't expect me to believe that just one girl at this party was doing something illegal and the rest weren't?"

The deputy mayor swung around and put his finger in Sam's face. "Just you see that you don't try to blame the city for this unfortunate accident. The mayor would not look kindly on anyone trying to discredit him or Bridgeway." He turned away and headed for the office door. "Bridgeway does not have a drug or alcohol problem. It was an accident, Louden. An unfortunate accident."

Sam watched the deputy mayor slam the door behind him as he left his office. *There goes one more ostrich with his head in the sand.*

✿

Mike paced the short length of the holding cell. He strained to hear the words of disconnected voices drifting from one of the many offices down the hall. The waiting was beginning to wear on him. He wasn't sure how much longer he could take of this trial.

A guard passed by the cell. "Take a load off, kid. You're making me tired just watching you."

"How much longer?"

"Not long now." The guard looked to one side then the other. Mike waited.

"I heard that the jury was getting real close to a decision. Shouldn't be much longer. You hang in there, kid."

Mike nodded and turned back to the empty cell. The stainless steel toilet and washbasin could be seen from whatever angle one wanted to look. The stale odor of sweat and mildew along with the faint odor of a pine cleaner made his stomach turn.

The wooden bench already proven too hard to sit on, instead he leaned against one of the graffiti covered walls and closed his eyes.

"Let's go kid."

Chapter Seventeen

"Katherine, here drink this."

Katherine's cold hands closed around a warm Styrofoam coffee cup.

Sam Louden stepped back just enough to give Katherine some space, but close enough to catch the cup if it should fall.

"Why, Sam?" Katherine turned a tear-stained face toward the man she'd put her faith in to bring her justice for her daughter's death. "Why would the jury say Mike wasn't guilty? Anna didn't take those drugs by herself, I know she didn't. Someone gave them to her. It had to have been Mike."

"I wish we'd been able to get more on Mike. The testimony of that Slater girl didn't help either. I couldn't shake her on the stand." Sam took a sip of his own cold coffee and grimaced. "The defense apparently cast enough doubt in the jury's eyes to keep them from returning a guilty verdict."

"Cast doubt? They cast stones! They made Anna out to be a horrible girl and Mike an innocent! How could the jury believe that?" Katherine's hands shook as she took a tentative sip of the hot coffee.

"We only had the facts to work with."

"Facts? What facts? Everything you said they twisted and turned until the real facts were lost."

"I know you're angry, Katherine. You have every right to be. Your daughter's death, though tragic, has been declared an accidental drowning by the authorities. Maybe you should take some time to grieve, huh?"

Deflated, like a spent balloon, Katherine slumped in the chair. "What do I do now?"

"Take some time off. Process your feelings. Then move on." Sam tried for a bit of levity. "I'm not the psychologist, you are."

Katherine didn't think his joke was that funny. "So much for being a psychologist. I'm not even sure about my own feelings anymore, how can I help someone else?"

"I'm sorry, bad job at injecting humor." Sam smiled, his eyes tinged with sadness. "I'm sorry, Katherine. I wish I could have done more."

"You did your best, Sam. I'm sorry for attacking you for something that was probably out of your hands anyway." Katherine placed the coffee cup on the edge of his desk. "I'm going to go."

"Are you going to be all right?"

"Yes, I'll be fine. Thank you." Katherine held out her hand.

Sam shook it then held it a bit longer. "If there's anything I can do for you, please let me know."

Katherine tightened her grip for a second then slowly withdrew her hand. "I will. Thank you."

"I mean it, Katherine. Any time."

"I have to get home. I promised my sister I'd call her when I found out the verdict."

～～

Katherine pulled her car into the garage and turned off the engine. She gathered her purse and suit jacket from the front seat then went inside.

As she turned off the alarm, the emptiness of the house surrounded her. She touched a switch and bright light filled the kitchen. It didn't help chase away the loneliness. It only helped her see that she really was alone.

She kicked off her shoes and walked in stocking feet to the refrigerator to pour herself a glass of juice. Glass in one hand and cordless telephone in the other; she curled up in a sofa chair to call her sister.

"Hi Maggie, it's me." Katherine spoke into the telephone.

"Katherine, we've been waiting for your call. How's the trial going?"

"It's over."

"Over? Has the jury reached a verdict?"

"Not guilty." Katherine sipped her juice trying to swallow past the lump in her throat.

"Oh honey, I'm so sorry. I know how much this meant to you."

"Not to me, Maggie, to Anna. I wanted to find a reason for her death. Those people act like she's just another statistic, but she isn't. She wasn't. She ... she ..." Katherine couldn't go on. She cried and poured out her heart to her older sister.

"I know, hon, just let it out." Maggie made shooshing noises into Katherine's ear.

"Her friends ... those kids she associated with ..." Katherine hiccupped. "No one came to Anna's defense." Blowing her nose on a tissue she continued, "Maggie, was I such a terrible mother? Was it my fault Anna turned to drugs and drinking?"

"Oh, Katherine, you don't think any of this is your fault do you? Hon, you may never know the truth about what happened that night. It's obvious those kids are going to keep the truth to themselves to protect one of their own."

"Maggie, I'm just so tired of it all." Katherine slumped into her chair, exhausted.

"I know hon. You have to get through this."

"I don't know if I can anymore."

"Yes, you can. You can do anything. I knew that when we were kids. You always hung in there longer than anyone else."

"Not anymore, Mags."

"Remember the time when we were at Grandma's and we had that bet about who could stay outside in the barn longest in the dark? You won! Remember our bet about who could stay up in Grandma's attic? You won. You can endure, Katie, you can do it."

"I'm not so sure anymore."

"Would you like me to come and stay with you for awhile?"

"No, you're needed there. I'll be all right. I just need to get some sleep."

"Are you having trouble sleeping?"

"To say the least. I close my eyes and I see her face. I can't seem to find any peace."

"Katherine, didn't the doctor give you something to help you sleep? Do you still have the pills?"

"There around here somewhere."

"Promise me you'll take one tonight and get some rest."

"I don't know, Maggie."

"Please, Katherine? You can't keep going like this. You're not a machine. You need to rest. You know how important it is to get enough hours of sleep."

"All right. I could never say no to you."

"That's a good girl. Now, do you have anything else you need to do tonight?"

"No, not really."

"Good, then go get those pills now and take them while you're on the phone with me."

"What? Don't you trust me?"

"I just know you. You'll get caught up in doing something else and never get around to it. Go. I'll wait."

Katherine's lips turned up at the corners as she looked at the telephone imagining her sister on the other end. She dragged herself into the kitchen and rummaged through the piled up mail on the counter until she found the small orange prescription bottle.

She twisted the white top off and shook out a tiny round white pill. She looked at it for only a second before popping it into her mouth and swallowing it with the last of her juice.

"All right, Maggie, I took the pill. Are you happy?"

"Yes, but it wasn't for me, Katie, it was for you. You go get comfortable and crawl into bed. Let that pill do its job."

"You know, that sounds like a good idea."

"Good. I'll call you tomorrow."

※※

"Yo, Mike. Come on. Let's go celebrate!" John called out to Mike from his car.

"Yeah, come on, Mike. We're all gonna head over to the beach and party." Amanda hung out the window.

"You guys go on without me, I'll catch up with you later." Mike hung back in the doorway.

"What's up with that, dude?"

"Yeah, Mike. Get your shit together and come with us now." Jessie opened the car door and scooted over to make room.

"I'm just not really in the mood, guys."

"Okay, that's it." Jessie crawled out from the backseat. She trotted across the lawn and grabbed Mike's arm. "We aren't going to take no for an answer."

"Jess, come on. Give me a break."

"No, you deserve to get out and have a good time." Jessie called into the living room. "Mr. Beckett, we're taking Mike to the beach. Be back later."

"Good idea. Get him out of the house."

"See, there you go. Now you have to go." Jessie pulled on Mike's arm.

"Okay, fine. If we're gonna party, we're gonna do it right." Mike slid into the backseat with Jessie. "Let's stop at Paul's on the way to the beach."

"All right! Now you're talking!"

John maneuvered the car through morning traffic and made it to Paul's apartment in a few minutes.

"You guys hang here, I'll be right back." Mike held out his hand. "Come on, ante up."

Money piled into Mike's outstretched hand. "Cool."

After Mike left, Jessie stretched out in the backseat and put her feet out the window. "Anybody notice Mike's been acting different since the trial?"

"Whadda mean?" John turned to glance at Jessie.

"You know, he should be jammin' and we had to practically twist his arm to get him to come with us."

"You know how Mike is." Amanda opened her compact to check her makeup. "He's still probably upset that Anna died."

"I guess, but ..."

"Oh give it up, little boy, Mike's not any different than usual." Amanda checked her makeup one last time then put her compact away.

Jessie reached over the headrest of the front seat and flicked the back of Amanda's head. "Don't call me a little boy again, or I'll—"

"You'll what?"

"All right you two, put away the claws." John caught Jessie's eye in the rearview mirror. *Don't go there*, his expression said to Jessie.

With a pout and a sigh, Jessie slouched into the backseat glaring daggers at the back of Amanda's head. "Stupid bitch." Jessie mumbled only loud enough for her to feel like she actually said it aloud. She knew John was right. This wasn't the time or place. They were there for Mike. But, as soon as Mike got over this funk he was in, she was going to let Amanda have it, right between the eyes. With a small smile to herself, Jessie let the image of Amanda knocked flat on her butt amuse herself while they waited for Mike.

"Yo, dude. Did you get the stuff?" John asked as Mike ambled back to the car.

"Hey, why don't you say it a little louder, jerk-off, I don't think the cops on the corner heard you."

"Up yours, smartass. Just get in the car." John started the car and gunned the engine.

John pulled the car onto the highway and followed the beach-going traffic down Gulf Boulevard. "Mike, let's get this celebration on the road. Pass me a smoke."

"Hang on, I don't have them rolled yet." Mike tossed a plastic bag to Jessie. "Here, hang onto this. I gotta get my papers out of my wallet."

"So, where should we park?" John asked.

Amanda placed a hand with bright red painted nails on John's arm and leaned over the console. "Why don't we head over to that park where the old fort is? It's quiet and not as crowded." She squeezed John's arm. "We might be able to find a little spot where we can have some privacy."

Irritated, Jessie kicked at the front seat repeatedly with her foot.

"Jess, you mind?"

"What?"

"I'm trying to drive."

"Yeah, so. Drive."

"Well, I could do it a lot better if you'd stop kicking my seat."

"Yeah? I bet you could do it a lot better if you didn't have someone hanging all over you."

"Mike? Hey dude, give Jessie something to do, will ya?"

"I don't need a babysitter."

Amanda laughed and flipped her hair back. "We shouldn't have brought the child. She's too young to party with us."

"I'll show you who's too young."

"Here, Jess, help me roll these." Mike interrupted.

"Yeah, no problem." Jessie turned to Mike and helped him roll several joints. She rummaged through the paper bag Mike brought back from Paul's apartment. "So, what other goodies did you bring us?"

Mike smacked her hand. "Get back. You'll find out when we get to the beach."

"Well, we're here, so let's pull it out." John parked the car beneath a palm tree close to the trail to the beach that led between the tall sea oats.

"Get the blanket out of the trunk, John. I don't want to sit in the sand." Amanda ordered as she slid out of the car.

"Yeah, John. Don't forget the princess's throne."

Mike giggled and casually draped an arm around Jessie's shoulder. "You're so bad."

It was all the encouragement Jessie needed. She wrapped her arms around Mike's neck and pulled his face close to hers. "You should see how bad I can really be," she whispered, her lips close to his. She pressed her small body into his arms.

"Well, we'll just have to see about that." Mike lowered his hands until he reached her small waist and picked her up.

Jessie squealed as her feet left the ground. She wrapped her legs around Mike's much stronger torso and spurred him on. "Last one to the beach is a rotten egg!"

The teenagers raced to a secluded spot on the beach away from the few tourists who lay in the sun and fell sprawled among the sand and crushed shells.

"Hurry, John and spread the blanket." Amanda stood and brushed bits of sand from her tanned thighs.

"Yeah, hurry John. Don't want Amanda to get sand on that bottled tan. She might streak." Jessie ducked instinctively as a towel came flying in her direction. "Thanks, I needed a towel to sit on." Jessie spread the towel out, sat on one end and patted the other to encourage Mike. He didn't need a second request. He sat on the end of her towel and pulled the ice chest toward him. After fishing two bottles of soda out of the rapidly melting ice, he opened each soda then poured out a portion.

"Hey, whadda do that for?" Jessie asked.

"Here hold these." Mike gave her the soda bottles. "Thought we could use a little flavor." He pulled out a small bottle filled with dark amber liquid.

"Oh," Amanda squealed. "Yummy! Rum!"

Mike and Jessie laughed as they worked together to keep from spilling as they poured rum into bottles of soda for each of them.

Along with the bottle of rum, they passed several joints among each other until they lay back on the sand in a semi-dozing state.

"I'm so stoned I can't move, dude." John half smiled at Mike who lay with his head in Jessie's lap.

"Yeah, me too." Mike shifted his head and Jessie's hand returned to continue smoothing his hair from his forehead. "That feels good, Jess."

"I guess you don't want me to stop then, right?" Jessie teased by holding her hand still.

"Not if you don't want me to tickle you." He showed her what he meant by running his fingers across her calves and down to her feet.

Jessie pushed her feet away from Mike's wandering fingers. "Okay, I give, you know how ticklish my feet are."

Amanda sighed as if tolerating the antics of spoiled children. She turned over to give the sun a chance to warm her backside. "Did you ever expect in a million years that our summer would start out like this?" she asked before dropping her face into the crook of her arm.

"No, but then no one ever really expects to be charged with murder." John said.

"You know what I mean." Amanda lifted her head to look at John. "I mean, come on, who would have ever thought that Anna would ever have anything but good luck her entire life?" Amanda sipped from her bottle of soda. "She was picked as most likely to succeed at, well, everything!"

"That's what life's all about, Mandy." Jessie interrupted. "A sequence of accidents. Anna was in the wrong place at the wrong time when life happened." Jessie looked at Mike to see if he was following the conversation.

"I wish I could be as accepting as you are about Anna's death."

"I'm not saying I'm over it, but if I dwell on it, then I'd just go crazy." She cast a furtive glance at Mike. "Besides, it was an accident." Jessie emphasized the word accident.

"Well, I learned one thing, not to combine swimming and drinking." Amanda brushed her hair back with a flip of her wrist.

"Did you even get in the pool at all that night, Amanda?"

"I didn't see you in the water." John muttered sleepily.

"Mike? Did you see Mandy in the water that night?" Jessie tapped Mike on the shoulder.

"What night?"

"You know, the night Anna drowned."

Mike turned over and hid his face in Jessie's lap. "I don't 'member much of that night."

"Not even—"

"I don't want to talk about it, okay?"

"Okay, let's change the subject."

Mike sat up and stared out at the breaking waves on the shore. They each stared in different directions. Mike watched seagulls dive at a couple of children playing close to the water. Jessie rested her chin on her knees and sifted sand through her fingers.

Once again, it was Amanda that broke the silence. "Hey, my dad's been reading your dad's articles and says to tell you he's rooting for your old man, whatever that means."

"It means that Mike's dad's been really giving it to the single mothers who let their kids run around without supervision." John said. He made a comical face and pointed his finger at himself.

Jessie laughed at his antics. "Yeah, John, like you. You should be the poster boy for bad single mothers."

"Thanks a lot, Jess."

"I'm sorry, it was meant in fun. You know what I mean." Jessie rushed on to cover the awkward silence. "Really, I wonder what Mr. Beckett would have to say if he ever met your mom?" Jessie asked.

"He doesn't need anymore ammunition. He'd have a field day with my old lady."

"It seems like he's really got it in for Anna's mom. Although, my dad says he never really comes out and gives names, but we all know who he's talking about." Amanda yawned and turned again. She shielded her eyes from the bright sun until she found her sunglasses.

"He's just doing his job." Mike muttered. "He'll go back to picking on city officials now that I'm home and this court shit is over." Mike sat up and faced the water. "He'll go back to ignoring me and forgetting all about me, same as before." Mike balled up a fist and shoved it into the sand. "Besides, he doesn't even care what I do, and I'm being raised by a single parent. Just not a single mom."

Jessie put her hand on Mike's shoulder. His muscles tightened. "Hey, don't say that. Look how hard your dad worked to keep you from going to jail."

Mike shrugged off her hand. "Uh huh. Right. And, now that I'm not worth mentioning in his precious column I'm not important enough for him."

"Well, at least he stays out of your life, not like my parents." Amanda said. "They're constantly trying to be one of my friends. They always try to get me involved in some event. They're always looking for stuff we can do together. It's so lame."

"Yeah, and mine's so busy with the other kids and their jobs and paying the bills that all they talk about is one more year until I graduate." Jessie sighed and lay face down on the towel.

John jumped up. "Hey, this is supposed to be a celebration party, not a pity party. Get up. Let's go explore the fort."

Chapter Eighteen

With Mike out with his friends, Charles Beckett stopped into his favorite bar for a nightcap after checking in at the office. He squinted and waited for his eyes to adjust before he took his usual stool at the end of the bar near the dartboard and away from the front door.

"Hey, Charlie, I saw your article this morning," the bartender called out.

"Yeah, what'd ya think?"

"Not bad. Not bad." The bartender pulled a tap and filled a frosted mug. He placed a napkin in front of Beckett and put mug of beer on the napkin.

"Hey, I read it too, you make some good points." A large bearded man slid down the bar to take the stool next to Beckett.

Beckett took a long drink of his beer before responding. "Yeah? What'd you like about it? You know, I'm always looking for honest opinions." He winked at the bartender as if they shared an inside joke.

"Well," the large man stroked his beard for a moment then said, "I think if more women stayed home and took care of the house and kids, we just might have a chance at regaining our moral values."

"Values and morals you say?" Beckett leaned back on his stool to look at the man who was eager to talk.

"Yeah. I mean, take me and my wife for example. I work hard and I expect dinner when I get home. Now, she ain't the greatest cook." He nudged Beckett with his large elbow. "Ain't nobody better than my ma, that goes without saying. But, my wife does a fair job. She keeps the kids in line when she has to, she takes care of the house and she makes sure my dinner is ready when I get home. Can't ask for better than that."

"I hear ya, man." The bartender wiped up the glass ring sweat from a previous customer and leaned an elbow on the bar.

Beckett laughed at the serious face of the bartender. For as long as he'd been coming here, Ray had never been married and probably never would be. He lived over his bar and ate, slept, and drank the bar business.

"He's pulling your leg, my friend. Ray here isn't even married."

Beckett slapped the big man on the back and motioned for Ray to refill their glasses.

"Well, if I was married ..." Ray let the sentence linger because he knew and he knew Beckett knew that it would never happen.

"What about you?" The big man turned to Beckett. "You married?"

"Divorced."

"Yeah? Too bad. What happened? She didn't know her place?" The big man laughed at his own joke.

"Something like that." Beckett drained his second beer and motioned for Ray to keep his glass filled. "Women tend to get in the way of having a good time."

"You don't usually want for female companionship, Charlie." The bartender said as he refilled Beckett's glass.

"No, not usually, Ray."

"I mean, last time you got that award for your writing, you had some tall blond hanging all over you when you stopped by."

"Oh, yeah, right. Sandra or Sondra or something like that." Beckett slapped the bar with his open palm. "Hell, she was something wasn't she? Little too clingy for my liking, though."

The large man excused himself and headed for the bathroom.

"So, Charlie, how's your kid?"

"Mike? He's doing okay. None the worse for wear I guess from going through this whole trial mess." Beckett twirled the glass in his hands. "He's out with his friends right now celebrating the end of the trial and his acquittal."

"It's too bad that girl had to die, but to go and blame it on your kid, that ain't right, ya know?"

"Yeah, I know. Just goes to show how far some people will go to blame others for their own problems."

The big man returned and settled his large frame back onto the barstool. "Who blames others for their problems?"

"Women." Beckett spat out the word as if it tasted bad in his mouth. "Women are always blaming someone or something else for their problems. They don't take responsibility for anything."

"If you ask me, they ain't cut out for handling big responsibilities anyhow."

Beckett looked at the big man.

"I mean, take my wife, she does just what she's told and we get along great." The big man boasted. "She don't spend nothing on nothing unless we discuss it first."

Beckett slapped him on the shoulder. "Lucky man." He picked up the darts from their wooden stand at the end of the bar. "Care for a game?"

"Sure, I'll play. Not much good at it, though."

"That's okay. I don't play for money."

Chapter Nineteen

Charles Beckett didn't give up on his campaign to smear Katherine Marshall or women in general. He spent the next week investigating Katherine Marshall's past in an attempt to personally discredit her profession and her parenting tactics.

He sat at his computer and stared at the screen saver of an animated underwater environment. A small nagging at the back of his mind made him stop and consider if he was doing the right thing.

He dedicated his newspaper column to pointing out the results of bad parenting and how it affected the children. The response was overwhelming. His editor encouraged him to continue based on the increase in ratings.

The editorial page gave equal time to those who wanted to write in and give their opinion of his column. The public opinion ranged from hearty agreements to heated battles about rising costs and two-family incomes to single parent woes.

He tapped the keyboard and the fish and sea critters disappeared. A blank word processing page appeared. Charles Beckett wasn't going to waste such a great opportunity. His next article would cover some of the topics he had been discussing on the radio last night.

He had received requests from the radio talk shows to express his opinions. Everyone wanted to ride the wave of success. His appearances on the radio gave him the chance to drive his message home. Women who don't take care of their family first end up alone. To further make his point, Beckett's rants included women in the counseling profession.

He wielded his virtual saber pen with a mighty hand. The rush of power to his ego was exhilarating. He knew the other writers envied his recent success.

He couldn't stop now, even if he wanted to. He'd gone too far to turn back.

Deftly, he managed to blanket the airwaves and newspapers with innuendoes and doubts that any woman who intended to provide advice to others in a professional capacity should consider their own family situation first. He cautioned his listeners and readers to consider carefully a counselor's own family history before entering into any session.

With his editor's help, he managed to stay just on the right side of libel and slander. Several times the newspaper's lawyers had to step in and re-work a sentence or two just to make sure they couldn't be sued, but other than that, they gave Beckett free reign to do as he pleased, so long as the ratings hike continued.

He felt a hand on his shoulder as he sat at his desk. "Beckett, we need to talk." He looked up to see his editor standing next to him.

"What's up Joe?"

"About tomorrow's column." Joe Splanto sat on the corner of Beckett's desk. He fingered the tie his daughter had given him for Father's Day a few weeks ago. "You're getting real close to the line and we need you to drop back a few degrees."

"Are you getting cold feet, Joe?"

"No, I'm not. It's just that we've been getting some letters to the editor that are beginning to worry the powers to be."

"Like what?"

"Like people claiming they saw Katherine Marshall not being a good mother and shit like that."

"Hey, I never named names in my column."

"Yeah, I know that. You know that. But, the big wigs in the corner office are leaning pretty heavy on me to get you to lay off."

"What would you do, Joe?"

"You already know the answer to that question, Beckett." Joe caught Beckett's eye and winked.

"Gotcha."

≈≈

Jennie hung up the telephone and went to stand in the doorway to Katherine's office. "Katherine, that's the fifth person to cancel in the last three days."

Katherine pushed her hair back from her face and laid the pen down she was using to make notations in a patient's file. "Yes, I know. I should have seen this coming."

"Seen what? Beckett writing scathing columns against you and your profession?" Jennie stomped her high-heeled foot. "He can't get away with this, can he?"

"I've checked with my lawyer and he says that the newspaper is being very careful by not naming names or anything else that can directly point to me."

"But, if your business is suffering directly because of what he says then can't we do something?"

"Did each person who cancel tell you it was because of something they read in the newspaper or heard on the radio?"

"Well, no of course not. They wouldn't say that. But, I can hear it in their voices."

"Jennie, I know how you feel, but we can't point fingers on supposition. Then we'd be no better than the newspaper." Katherine was careful not to place blame on Beckett. She'd already had enough finger pointing as it was. "Besides, who says that they aren't right?"

"Huh?" Jennie couldn't believe her ears.

"I've been doing a lot of thinking lately. Maybe I should just use this opportunity to take some time off. I'm not really myself yet. I'm tired all the time. My patience is wearing thin." She smiled slightly at her small joke.

"You're not just going to give up, are you?"

"I don't call it giving up. I just don't think I should be treating patients if I'm not capable of keeping my own life under control."

"But, Anna's death wasn't your fault!"

"Jen, listen to me. It's the doubts I have about myself that are forcing me to make this decision."

Jennie bounced the toe of her shoe against the bottom of the doorjamb. "Look, today is Wednesday, why don't you just take a long weekend and things will be brighter on Monday, okay?"

"Maybe. We'll see." Katherine turned to her desk and picked up her appointment book. "Why don't you refer my active patients to Dr. Jeffries, but check with their insurance companies first. The rest of them, check to see when their evaluations are scheduled and if we can wait, put them aside. The others, ask them to reschedule for ..." She flipped the pages of her appointment book. "... three months from now. If that's possible. If they can't wait, ask them if they'd like to be referred to another therapist." Katherine closed her appointment book and slid it into a desk drawer.

"You're serious, aren't you?" Jennie asked.

"Yes, I am. I'm sorry, Jennie. I know you were depending on me and this job, but I don't seem to be very dependable right now."

"Right now, I could care less about being out of a job, it's you I'm worried about." Jennie reached out a hand to Katherine. "I'm here for you."

"I appreciate it, I do." Katherine tried to smile.

"Not everyone in this town is against you."

"I know. It just seems like it."

"You've got to fight this horrible treatment."

"Jen, right now I just want to go home and try and get some sleep. I haven't been sleeping well lately."

"I can imagine."

"I hope you don't ever have to." Katherine packed her briefcase and stood. "I guess that's it. Can you handle the rest?"

"Yeah, don't worry about it. I'll finish calling your patients and making the arrangements. And, if we have to go through their insurance companies, I'll take care of that too."

"Jen, I don't want to you be out of a job. I still want you to come in a few days a week and take care of messages, referrals, and whatever comes up. I'll call Dr. Jeffries and let him know that you'll be referring patients to his office. If there's an emergency, he can contact me. But, I doubt he'll need to. He's more than capable of handling anything that may come up."

"Maybe you might want to stop in and talk to him?"

"We'll see. I'll check if he has time to talk to me." Katherine hid her face as she reached a hand into her bag pretending to search for her keys. "Well, I guess that's it. The office is yours to run."

"Katherine, call me if you need anything."

"Sure thing, Jen."

Katherine knew Jennie wanted to hug her so she stepped forward and gave the girl a hug. She'd stuck with her through this entire situation. Jennie was a good girl and a heck of an assistant. "Don't worry. I'm not running away. I'm just recharging my batteries."

Jennie laughed. "I'm going to hold you to that statement." She hugged Katherine again. "If you're not back here soon I'll send the National Guard to get you."

Katherine thought about Jennie's statement as she parked her car in the garage and let herself into her empty house. The National Guard just might be what it would take to drag her out of her mood. She was a licensed therapist with a degree in psychology. She knew better than anyone else what was happening to her. How could she possibly treat her patients when she couldn't even treat herself?

Katherine tossed her briefcase and purse onto a chair and kicked off her shoes. She collapsed on the sofa and let the tears that she'd been holding back all day fall unchecked.

Chapter Twenty

Katherine wandered about the house in a same pair of old sweat pants and t-shirt she'd been wearing for several days. She'd refused to pick up the paper from the front door step, even though, Nick, the lawn guy had been kind enough to move the pile from the end of her driveway to the front door.

She used her answering machine to screen all calls and only took those from her sister or Jennie. Grateful that they didn't call often, Katherine spent most days in a sleepy fog and most nights pacing the halls of the big empty house.

The television barely held her interest but it was a great escape. Questions nagged her night and day about Anna's death. She argued with herself about whether she had been a good mother and a good role model.

Walking through the hall and past the front door she stumbled over the pile of mail accumulating beneath the mail slot. She knelt down to pick it up. "Oh God." Katherine cried as she fell onto the cold tile and curled up holding a copy of the *Seventeen* magazine she'd forgotten to cancel.

The teenage model's bright cheerful face grinned happily at her from the cover of the magazine. Katherine stroked the shiny magazine cover. "Oh, Anna. What happened to my baby?"

Taking a deep breath, Katherine forced herself to get up. She gathered the rest of the mail and moved it to a counter in the kitchen.

Feeling the need to be close to her daughter, Katherine made her way to her daughter's room. She hadn't been in there since the day before her death. When it had come time to choose a dress for her funeral, Katherine had left the task to her sister.

She opened the door of her daughter's room. Tears coursed down her cheeks as she inhaled the still present fragrance of her daughter's favorite body spray. Katherine picked up a pillow off Anna's bed and breathed deep of the floral scent. She sat on her daughter's bed and gathered an armful of the Beanie Babies strewn about. She hugged them close.

"Anna, I know you were a good girl. I'm so sorry I couldn't protect you." She whispered into the toys she held close.

"I can't do this. I can't!" Katherine moaned to herself. She put the stuffed toys back on the bed, smoothed the bedspread over the pillows and left the room. Exhausted, she fell into bed and cried herself to sleep.

The next morning, Katherine rose with a renewed purpose. She hurried to wash away the grime and grit from not showering for days. After a small breakfast of juice and a banana she gathered a variety of empty boxes from the garage and carried them to Anna's room.

"Come on, Katherine," she told herself, "you can do this." Katherine opened the door to Anna's room and stepped once again into her daughter's room.

She started by filling a box with the menagerie of stuffed animals strewn about the room. It went easier than she thought, although as she emptied the dresser drawers of Anna's clothes it was hard for her not to remember the last time Anna wore each item of clothing.

It took all of her strength to keep filling the boxes. Deep in her heart she knew that the circumstances surrounding Anna's death meant more. "Anna, speak to me, please." She begged the silent room. "Tell me why you took those drugs."

Sadness settled over Katherine. She knew she had to accept the accident that claimed her daughter's life and find some kind of closure. The psychological implications were obvious to her. Using the techniques she had provided her patients was harder to accept. She didn't have the strength to fight the overwhelming grief.

After a brief rest and snack she tackled Anna's closet. Shoes, magazines, papers, books, and empty soda cans fell out onto the floor when she opened the closet door.

"So that's what she does with her stuff when I ask her to clean her room."

Katherine sorted the garbage from the rest of the closet contents. She piled library books onto the bed making a mental note to return them the next time she was on that side of town. She discovered an assortment of clothes and shoes she'd never seen her daughter wear. They were skimpier and more revealing than anything she would have approved of for her daughter's wardrobe. At first, Katherine resisted the idea of her daughter wearing the outfits. She hoped that they belonged to any one or more of the other girls that Anna hung out with on a regular basis. But, doubts nagged at the back of her mind. The doubting grew stronger when she pulled a box from the corner of the closet and found notebooks filled with her daughter's handwriting.

Could these be her daughter's diaries? Katherine's hands shook as she slowly removed them from the box. She sat on the edge of Anna's bed and ran her fingers over the pen drawings on the outside. *Anna loves Mike. Mikes loves Anna. Anna and Mike 4ever.* Chunky letters ran together into familiar symbols, symbols that Katherine had seen on spray painted fences and outside walls of businesses. "Gang insignia?" Katherine spoke the words aloud then dropped the notebook as if it had burned her fingers.

Running from the room, Katherine didn't stop until she was outside standing next to the pool. She breathed deep gulping breaths of air. Feeling faint, she leaned over and placed her hands on her knees.

Who was this girl she'd been calling her daughter all these years? What kind of life was she living outside her home? Why hadn't she seen any of this? How could she have been so blind? Was she really the horrible parent who cared more about her job than her family life that Beckett implied in his column?

Katherine dropped onto the soft cushioned seat of the matching patio furniture and let her head drop back against the small headrest. It wasn't until the sun had nearly disappeared from the sky and the mosquitoes were becoming a nuisance that she awoke from her trance-like state and went back into the house to fall mentally exhausted into bed.

On the third morning of cleaning her daughter's room, Katherine managed to pack the rest of Anna's clothes into the remaining boxes. She threw away magazines, makeup, and several other bags of trash. Music CDs filled another box along with a compact stereo, a portable CD player, and headphones. Katherine spent nearly two hours tearing posters off the walls and removing tape and staples from the wallpaper. Deciding to re-paper the walls instead of salvaging what was left, she stripped wallpaper along with the posters of boy bands and television stars.

Katherine worked in silence until all that was left was the bed, dresser, desk with computer, and the notebooks she had dropped on the floor the day before.

She had purposely left the notebooks for last, hoping to avoid the words inside for as long as possible. The inevitable had been postponed long enough. With a bottle of chardonnay, Katherine gathered the notebooks and carried them into her bedroom. She crawled into bed, opened the first graffiti-covered notebook, sipped her wine, and began reading.

Early the next morning, the wine bottle long emptied, Katherine closed the last page on the last journal entry her daughter made. It was dated the night before she drowned. Katherine closed her eyes, imagining her daughter laying across her bed scribbling into her notebook. "Tomorrow night I'm going to tell Mike that I want to break up. I'm afraid of what he's going to say or do. I'm hoping to get accepted by the college in CA. I don't want to have Mike hanging all over me when I go away. He's gonna freak, I just know it."

Katherine's mind reeled with all that she had read. *Did Mike freak as Anna wrote in her journal? Was the jury wrong in claiming he wasn't guilty for Anna's death?*

Unable to sleep, Katherine paced first her bedroom, then the rest of the house. Overloaded with new insight, she felt a chill run through her body. She'd discovered a new, dark side to her child's life. She'd learned more than any parent should ever have to about her child's private life.

According to Anna's journal she had feared she was pregnant several months ago. Pregnant! Katherine shuddered. What else had Anna kept from her?

Katherine stopped pacing and raced to Anna's room. She didn't hesitate at the door like she had before. She flung the door open and crossed the carpet that was no longer scattered with shoes, books, music CDs, or toys. She stood in front of the desk contemplating the computer screen. Her hands shook as she pulled the chair back and sat down. She pushed her hair back behind her ears and switched the computer on.

When Katherine could take no more of e-mails filled with four-letter words, sexual content, and brazen suggestions, she printed out all files she thought were relevant for Sam Louden's reading. She checked the clock to see if it was too early to call the assistant district attorney's office. Shocked, Katherine dialed the telephone shaken to see it was nearly noon. She'd been awake for thirty-six hours.

"District Attorney's office."

"Sam Louden, please."

"One moment, may I tell him who's calling?"

"Katherine Marshall." As she waited, Katherine rummaged in the refrigerator for a soda and something to eat.

"Sam Louden, here."

"Sam, it's Katherine Marshall. I hope I didn't interrupt anything important, but I really need to talk to you. I've found something here in Anna's room that I think you might be interested in."

"Sure, Katherine. Is it something we can go over on the telephone or do you want to come into the office?

"I guess I don't want to go over it on the phone, but if you could come out to the house, I'd appreciate it."

"Sure no problem. Let me check my schedule. All right, I can manage about an hour around 7:30 tonight. Is that all right?"

"Yes, that's great. I really appreciate this, Sam."

"Sure. Are you okay?"

"I don't know. I was hoping you could help me with that."

"Okay Katherine. You've peaked my curiosity. I'll see you tonight."

"Thank you, Sam."

Katherine hung up the telephone and hurried to gather Anna's journals and the stack of paper from the computer's printer. She carried them to the dining room and tried to organize them in some semblance of order. She felt a renewed energy surge through her body. Unable to sleep, her nerves a jangled mess, she puttered around the house, cleaning and straightening as she waited for the assistant district attorney's arrival.

At 7:35 Katherine opened her front door and welcomed Sam Louden into her home.

"Thanks for coming, Sam."

"Your call intrigued me, Katherine." Sam shook out his umbrella before setting it into the ceramic umbrella holder to drip.

"I've made a pot of coffee. Unless you want something a little stronger?"

"Coffee sounds great, thanks."

Katherine led the way into the dining room and motioned Sam to sit in one of the ornately carved mahogany chairs. She sat in another. "I guess I'll just get right to it. As I was cleaning Anna's room, I discovered her journals." Katherine stopped talking and looked away from Sam's face. "She ... I ..." she couldn't go on and was suddenly embarrassed about how to bring the subject up. "We need coffee." She jumped up from her seat at the table and rushed to the kitchen to gather cups and assorted sundries onto a tray. She busied herself pouring coffee and stirring in sugar and cream. She tapped her spoon on the side of the ceramic cup then laid it carefully on a linen napkin.

Unwilling to start talking again, she kept quiet while Sam stirred his coffee and took his first sip.

"Katherine, you didn't invite me over to just have coffee."

"No, I guess I didn't. She pulled a stack of papers to her, shuffled through them, and then pushed a few papers toward Sam. "Read this."

She fiddled with her coffee spoon while she kept her eyes on Sam as he read the e-mails.

"Did Anna write these?"

"From what I can figure, she wrote those on top." Katherine pushed more computer printed papers toward Sam. "These others where written by various people who she corresponded with." The last stack of papers she pushed to the side. "And, these were written by Mike Beckett."

Sam motioned for Katherine to push that stack of papers toward him and he read the first few e-mails. He whistled low and long after the first message. "Holy shit."

"My sentiments exactly."

"Have you read through all of this?"

"At least a dozen times." Katherine sorted through the journals and showed Sam several tagged entries.

"Here and here, Anna references possibly being pregnant, taking a pregnancy test, then telling Mike." She flipped a few pages and showed Sam where she cross-referenced to e-mails. "This e-mail from Mike is obviously in response to Anna telling him she might be pregnant. Look here ... he's angry. He tells her that she'd better take care of it and make it go away. Look, see, his words." Katherine pointed to the e-mail and repeated, "make it go away."

Sam studied the journals and e-mail entries. "Katherine, I'm not a psychologist, I'll leave that for you to interpret, but can you actually believe that the things these kids write about really happened? What about all these wild parties they talk about? Where could these have happened? What about these other kids' parents?"

"It's unbelievable, I know. But it's all I have right now."

"Did you ever notice bruises on Anna?"

"You know, looking back, I seem to remember times when Anna had bruises on her legs and maybe on her arms. But, she just shrugged them off, saying she fell in gym class or something or other. I never pushed her about it. I didn't expect that Mike or anyone else had hit her."

"Well, according to these journal entries it looked as if Mike abused her on a regular basis."

Katherine laid her head on her arms and blew out a heavy sigh. "God, Sam, How could I have been so blind to my daughter's life?"

"Don't blame yourself."

"Who else is there to blame? I should have been there for her. She obviously needed me and I wasn't there." Katherine refilled Sam's coffee cup and then her own.

"Not necessarily, look at these entries. She says that she was purposely keeping her problems from you."

"Right, but did you read why she was keeping her life from me?" Katherine flipped the pages of Anna's journal. "Read this. She says that she felt enormous pressure from me to be perfect. According to Anna I created this perfect life that was so different from my own childhood." She slammed her hands on the table making the spoons jump. "How could I do this to my own daughter? I'm such a horrible parent!" She turned to Sam. "Is there anything in here that we can use to get a new trial against Mike? Don't these statements from Anna about Mike hitting her make a difference?"

"Well, that's the thing, Katherine." Sam pushed the papers and notebooks aside and reached for his coffee cup. He grimaced as he sipped the tepid liquid. "Our judicial system frowns upon trying a defendant twice for the same crime." He reached for the coffee pot to refill his cup. "It's called double jeopardy."

"Why can't you charge him with something else?"

"Katherine, listen to me." Sam took her hand and stopped it from tapping aimlessly on the table. "The state took a chance and tried to get a conviction of third degree murder."

"But ..."

"But," Sam interrupted Katherine, "the fact is we'll probably never know what really happened that night. The reality is that something unfortunate happened and your daughter paid with her life. The combination of drugs, alcohol, and teenagers ended up being a lethal mixture."

Chapter Twenty-One

After Sam Louden left, Katherine changed for bed. Even though she hadn't slept for two days she wasn't all that tired. Instead, she spent the evening laying in bed staring at the ceiling while she thought about her own childhood. She tried to remember any times she shared with her mother. None came to mind. As a matter of fact, she couldn't recall any time at all when she and her mother shared a close moment.

She considered the similarities of her childhood and Anna's. Even though her father hadn't died like Anna's father, he was gone enough to make his absence significant. If her mother's reaction was any indication, her father could have been dead. Her mother's abusive, alcoholic rages raced to the forefront of her memory. The last time she'd talked to her mother was so many years ago she'd forgotten the actual number. Katherine recalled her high school graduation ceremony and her mother's obnoxious drunken blubbering scene in front of her friends. It had been the last straw. Katherine recalled harsh words being flung from both of them as she packed a bag to leave as quickly as possible. Her scholarship for college had been her saving grace.

She'd made a few halfhearted attempts at reconciling with her mother but it never worked out. Anger and impassioned arguments only made the moments together worse.

Katherine bolted from the bed unable to sit still. She paced back and forth across the room clenching and unclenching her hands.

Could it be true that her lack of a loving relationship with her own mother be what prevented her from having a healthy, real relationship with Anna? Had she really placed so much pressure on Anna to be perfect? Of course she had. Katherine smacked her forehead with the palm of her hand. She had entirely missed the fact that she had been too idealistic about the relationship she should have been cultivating with her daughter that she didn't actually follow through. She'd been so busy telling everyone that they had the perfect relationship that she didn't bother to actually work at making it happen.

How could she have been so blind? So stupid? So absolutely horrible to her daughter? She fell across the bed and buried her face into her pillow. *Oh, Anna. Please forgive me. I'm so sorry.* Katherine moaned into her pillow. *I failed you. I failed you. I tried too hard to make sure I didn't end up like my mother. I wanted to give you more than I ever had. I wanted to be the best provider. I'm so sorry.*

Exhaustion finally took its toll. Katherine cried herself to sleep and didn't waken for many hours.

Uncovering forgotten memories of her parents triggered a breakthrough for Katherine. When she awoke it was to a renewed purpose. Peacefulness settled over her like a soft blanket. Her first telephone call was to her sister to talk about her enlightenment.

"Maggie, I'm so ashamed of myself."

"Katie, don't be so hard on yourself, no one has a secret handbook for being a perfect parent."

"But, I should have known better."

"Why? Because you're a psychologist and trained in behavioral therapy?

"Well, yes."

"That's a load of crock."

"Margaret!"

"It's true. When you got your license to practice did they give you a special crystal ball so you can tell what's going on in your own family?"

"Of course not."

"Exactly. You're human, just like the rest of us."

"But, I should know better."

"Why?"

"Because I should."

"Katie, I love you. But, you can be dense sometimes."

"Hey, wait a minute—"

"I mean it. Haven't you ever heard of the old saying, the cobbler's children wear no shoes?"

"All right. You got me. For the first time in a long time I'm in a good mood."

"I'm so glad to hear it. I knew you'd pull through."

"I understand now that our father didn't stay away from home because he didn't love us, it was because he wanted to avoid all the stress at home."

"You have to stop taking responsibility for dad's leaving. And, Katherine ..."

"Yes?"

"You're going to have to stop blaming mom too."

"But, daddy wouldn't never have ..."

"Yes, he would. Daddy was having an affair with a woman in Springfield. Why do you think he kept the same route and didn't take those promotions?"

"I don't know. I guess I never really thought about what he could have been doing. I always thought he left because of mom's drinking."

"Mom started drinking when she found out about his affair, not because he was away all the time. Then again, it could have been for both reasons. Alcoholism is a disease, Katie."

"I've been such an idiot. I'm a bad daughter and a bad mother. What else did I do wrong? Have I been a horrible sister too?"

"No, Katie-bug, you haven't been a bad sister. You're not a bad mother or daughter either."

"I tried so hard not to be like mom that I prevented Anna and me from ever having a real relationship."

"I think Anna understood."

"Not from what I read in her journals she didn't."

"Katie, you have to give her the benefit of the doubt now. You may not be able to make it up to her ..."

"Wait, you might have something there."

"What'd I say?"

"I can make it up to her."

"How?"

"By helping other teenagers. Anna wasn't the only one in this town doing drugs and drinking. The whole crowd she hung out with did. At least according to her journals and the e-mails they passed back and forth. They're practically screaming out for help."

"Katie, you're such a good person. Are you sure you can handle this so soon after Anna's death?"

"I want to, Mags. I have to."

"What about mom?"

"I can't... Not yet. Give me some more time."

"I understand. But Katie?"

"Yes?"

"Don't wait too long. Mom isn't getting any younger and, well ..."

"I know."

Chapter Twenty-Two

Katherine smiled as she hung up the telephone. Smiling wasn't enough of an outlet for the joy she felt. She managed a small happy dance and even clicked her heels twice, before she calmed down enough to really consider her decision.

She'd called the high school principal and managed to convince her to let Katherine volunteer at the high school several days a week when school started in August. Katherine would be presenting various anti-drug and alcohol programs as well as seeing any teenager on an individual basis for counseling on any topic or concern the teenager may have.

It was a major coup for Katherine, but one she felt compelled to do. She let the principal's words wash over her again, "I think this a wonderful gesture on your part, Mrs. Marshall. We're lucky to have people like you in our community willing to share their knowledge and services with our youngsters."

Katherine had thanked her profusely for the chance. The principal's next suggestion is what prompted the happy dance on the kitchen tile. "Mrs. Marshall, why don't you start out small, and come down to the school during the end of the summer classes. We have a few students who could benefit greatly from your counseling services."

Katherine knew that it was meant to be a trial period. The school would have to check her credentials and verify her references, but it was a start. That's all she wanted. She got her chance. It was up to her to make sure she made the most of her opportunity by helping as many teenagers as she could.

She knew it was going to be rough at first. The kids would probably be resistant to her anti drug programs. Most teenagers were. But, if she could reach just one child and help them turn their life around it would all be worth it.

For the next week, Katherine spent every night in front of her computer pouring over websites and sending inquiries to the various national anti-drug and alcohol programs. She laughed when she told Jennie that she'd covered the entire alphabet forward and backward when it came to the many organizations.

Katherine's entire perspective on life has given her a renewed purpose. For the first time since Anna died, she considered the possibility of having a real purpose in life. Her telephone calls to her sister were becoming almost a daily ritual.

"Mags, I truly believe that this is my purpose in life."

"Honey, I believe you."

"I questioned the tragedies that have happened in my life. I've been so selfish only thinking of what was happening to me."

"That's only natural."

"Maybe so, but I needed to look beyond my own selfish needs."

"So, what have you come up with?"

"I am going to help teenagers. I'm going to dedicate my time to providing them with a place to go where they can be themselves. Where they can get accurate information. Where they can be safe."

"That's a big task for just one person."

"I know. I'm working on getting help. I have to start somewhere, right?"

"True."

"Anna's death will not have been for nothing. She will be remembered. I'll make sure of that."

"If anyone can do it, I know you can. Your decision didn't surprise me."

"Thanks."

"You're welcome."

"Hey, Mags, can I ask you a question?"

"Sure. What's up?"

"Did your kids ever keep diaries and if so, did you ever read them?"

"Well, I think all kids keep a diary at one time or another. If not a diary, they write their thoughts down on paper. Probably girls more than boys. And, yes, Sarah kept a diary. Several of them, as a matter of fact."

"Did you ever read it?"

"Well, there's been a couple of times that Sarah left her diary on her bed when she went to school. And, she knew that I would be going in there to make beds and pick up dirty clothes. I think she left it there on purpose for me to see."

"What did you find out?"

"She was confused about this boy she was dating. She was feeling some pressure about having sex. She wrote about it in her diary and probably expected me to see it that morning."

"So what happened?"

"Well, when she got home from school, I took her aside, we had a long talk about love and sex and when it was right between two people. I didn't mention ever reading her diary, and she didn't mention that she was thinking about having sex with her boyfriend."

"So, after you found out that Sarah kept a diary, did you search it out on a regular basis to find out what was going on in her life?"

"No. I respected her privacy. Not that it didn't drive me crazy, mind you. But, I had to have faith in my daughter that for the really tough decisions she would find a way to ask me."

"So you had this unspoken code?"

"You could say that. Every once in a while, I'd find her diary open on her bed and I knew she was reaching out to me. It was her way of letting me know what was troubling her."

"That's so great."

"Yeah, it was. But, we've moved beyond the diary communication. Now, she has no problem coming to me. But, her questions are about colic, skinned knees, and how to get a toddler to eat something other than peanut butter sandwiches."

Katherine laughed then went very quiet.

"I'm sorry, hon. I didn't mean to bring up ..."

"Oh, don't worry about it. I have to adjust. It'll be okay."

Lightning flashed and lit up the room. Katherine jumped as the thundering boom echoed rolled endlessly in the distance.

"I heard that thunder, isn't it hurricane season there?"

"Yeah, but nothing to worry about. This is just a normal summer storm. We had a few tropical storms drift up from the Caribbean but other than that, nothing serious."

"I worry when I hear about the storms on the news."

"Nothing to worry about. It's still early. Besides, we're over on the west coast. We don't get as many hurricanes on this side."

"You take care of yourself, Katie."

"I will. Say hello to Hank and the kids."

❦❦

The next morning at the office, Katherine told Jennie about her new plan.

"I think this is great, Katherine."

"I hope so. It's going to mean a lot of changes around here and we'll probably be putting in a lot more hours."

"You mean more than we already have?" Jennie put her notepad on her lap and gave Katherine a smile.

"You're a regular comedian, aren't you?"

"I try. So, what's this big plan?"

"I've gotten the okay to volunteer at the high school. I'm going to start with the summer school on a trial basis and if all goes well, I'll be on-site as a behavioral counselor for the coming school year."

"Hey, that's great!"

"It's going to mean a lot of extra work for you."

"I can handle it."

"I know you can. You've been great. Especially taking over managing the office while I was ... uh, out, taking some time off."

"You look much better."

"Thanks. I guess I was in pretty bad shape, huh?"

"Well, let's just say you could have passed for a walking zombie."
Katherine laughed. "I wasn't all that bad, was I?"

Jennie laughed along with Katherine. "Bad enough."

"But, this is only the start, Jennie. I'm going to be working after
hours too, or I should say, we are going to be working. I want to offer
free group counseling sessions for parents. Most parents don't understand what teenagers are going through and the strong pressure they're
under when it comes to drug and alcohol use."

"You're right about that."

"The signs of abuse can be so slight, most parents won't even
know. I mean, look at Anna. I didn't have a clue. And, I'm a trained
professional."

"But, that wasn't your fault, Katherine."

"In a way it was. I didn't see because I didn't want to. I have to
educate other parents about the signs of drug abuse, depression, and
even physical or sexual abuse."

"Kids need to know where to go if they want help too, being at the
high school could help."

"I hope so."

A small bell tinkled from the outer office. Jennie jumped up from
her chair and headed for the door. "That'll be your 1:30 appointment."

"Great. Give me five minutes to review her file then send Mrs.
Wallace in."

"Sure thing." Jennie turned back to face Katherine. "Hey, I think
you're doing a great thing."

"Thanks, Jennie. This is just the beginning. I have big plans for
the mental health of this community."

Jennie turned on her heel and headed out to greet Mrs. Wallace.
Before she left, she said, "Bridgeway, you better watch out!"

✍ ❧

"Mrs. Marshall?"

Katherine looked up from the small desk she'd been given to use
during summer school. A petite, dark haired girl hovered just within
the doorway. She looked like she would run at the first hint of trouble.
"Hi. Come in."

The girl sat on the edge of the folding chair across from Katherine's
desk. She put her backpack on the floor but kept glancing at the doorway. "I ..." she hesitated. "I have this friend."

"What's your friend's name?"

"No names."

"Okay, what do you want to talk about?"

"I'm not sure. I heard what you said today in class." The girl stumbled over her words, speaking softly. "My friend really needs to hear what you said. You know, about drinking."

"Do you have a friend who drinks too much?"

"Yeah. A lot. Way too much."

"Where does she get it?"

"Oh, you know. Older kids. Her parents' house. Places like that."

"You think she needs help?"

"Yeah."

"Do you want to take her some of these pamphlets?" Katherine motioned to the various anti-drinking information piled up on her desk and on the small table next to her chair.

"I dunno. She might. She might not."

Katherine picked up a few pieces of literature and slid them across the desk to the young girl. "Here. Why don't you take these? If your friend is interested in learning more she can come see me. I'd be happy to talk to her."

"Thanks." The girl shifted in her seat, reached for the pamphlets, then shoved them into her backpack.

For the rest of her short time at the school, Katherine sat in her small closet-like office, meeting with few students, spending more time organizing and re-organizing the anti-drug and alcohol literature she received from assorted organizations. They had all been eager to offer their literature and information for the asking.

She locked up the tiny office at the school and headed for her other office across town. She checked her watch to see if she had time to zip through a fast food drive-thru before her next group counseling session. Barely. Katherine pulled her car in line behind a minivan full of bouncing children.

Children jumping around without car seats or seatbelts. Doesn't that parent know the risks she's taking with her children's lives?

Katherine laughed at herself. *Good going. Take on another crusade, why don't you? You have some spare time between 2 am and 4 am where you're not doing anything special, like sleeping.*

While she waited for her burger and fries Katherine considered the group of parents she would be meeting with when she got back to her office. Most were single parents with teenage daughters. The parents were concerned about their daughters being involved in co-dependent relationships.

With Katherine's help and some well-developed intervention techniques, she hoped to provide the parents with the ability to help their daughters. It would take time, commitment, and energy. Much of which Katherine was borrowing, depending on her dedication to keep her going. It didn't matter how exhausted she was when she fell into bed each night. At least being so tired meant the nightmares were kept at bay.

If she could help just one parent, just one teenager it was all worth it.

Chapter Twenty-Three

Katherine drove into the parking lot at the local library and searched for a parking spot. She knew she was late. Nearly every slot was taken. She'd finally found a spot near the back of the parking lot when she'd all but given up and was going to park on the side of the road.

The newspaper ad reported that the city council hearing was public this evening. On a whim, she gathered all of her research papers and handouts and hurried to make the meeting time. She wanted to be near the front of the room when the speaker turned the floor over to questions and new business, but from the look of the cars in the parking lot, it was going to be a big crowd.

She almost turned around and raced back to her car when she walked into the meeting room and met the eyes of the other people who chose to attend the meeting. It had only been a couple of weeks since she'd reopened her office and she'd lost a few of her patients to Dr. Jeffries. She expected it to happen. The columns in the newspaper hadn't let up. Charles Beckett no longer used every moment to slam her, but he still managed to devote at least one column or the majority of one column to single women and examples of their supposed bad parenting tactics. She'd worked hard to keep her practice open. She'd even offered free group counseling classes for parents and teenagers. Volunteering at the high school had paid off too. Earlier this week she'd managed to help a young girl start on the road to recovery from alcoholism. It had been a tenuous relationship, but one that she'd managed to maintain, even after summer school ended.

Katherine glanced about catching others among the crowd whispering behind hands and pointing. She shrugged it off. After tonight, she hoped that they'd be receptive to her suggestions and welcome her back into the community with open arms.

Katherine raised her hand first when the question was raised for new business. As soon as she was recognized she spoke, "I'd like to suggest that the town build a recreational center for teenagers."

Laughter filled the room. Katherine went on, "I think the teenagers of this town need a safe, non-threatening place where they can gather in a neutral environment. Someplace where they can find refuge and advice. A place—"

"Do you know how much something like that would cost?"

"Well, no, not exactly, but ..."

"What about finding qualified people to run it?"

Katherine winced. That was obviously from someone who wasn't on her side. "I'd offer my services. And, I'm sure there are other parents and adults in the community who would volunteer their time as mentors."

"Are you implying that we have so many problem teenagers that they need a special place?"

"No, not exactly, but I've been doing a lot of volunteer work at the high school and it seems to me that they need a place to go where they can stay active and not have a lot of idle time to get into trouble."

"Just a lot of hogwash if you ask me. What these kids need are jobs not another daycare center."

"It wouldn't be a daycare center, sir." Katherine faced her accuser. "These teenagers don't need babysitters. They need information. They need advice."

"Why can't they go to their parents?"

Katherine turned to the woman who asked her question. "Did you go to your parents when you had questions or did you ask your friends or rely on urban myths?"

The woman found something very interesting in her lap and didn't respond.

"What about the rest of you parents," Katherine continued, "how many of you have had a serious conversation with your teenager lately?"

"It's the school's job to educate our kids."

"Yeah, that's right. The school has a program for these kids. They have sex education, drug education, and counselors. I think that our tax dollars prove that we're doing our share."

Katherine couldn't believe her ears. These people were supposed to care about their community and the lives of the members. Instead, they were looking for excuses to avoid responsibility.

Rev. Leo Swift stood up. Until then, he'd kept quiet. "Seems to me that we do have a bit of a drug problem among our teenagers. Kids get a lot of misinformation about drugs and don't understand the true ramifications of long-term abuse. I think that we should look to our schools and our churches and to the parents to provide the type of education these young folks need." He cleared his throat and tried not to look in Katherine Marshall's direction. "Most of all, I think that until Big Business steps out of the way of running this country, we aren't going to be able to take control of our youngsters. If we can't tear them away from this satanic rap music and those God-awful television shows, then we won't have a chance with a community center. We need to start small, then work our way outward into the community."

"Thank you, Reverend." The man banging the gavel managed to

control the room again with only a few whacks against the podium. "All right folks, settle down. We're about done here." He turned to Katherine Marshall. "Mrs. Marshall, we appreciate your coming tonight and offering a suggestion for a teenage community center. However, I think we'll have to give it more thought and consideration. Could you prepare a stronger case for the next meeting?"

"I suppose I could. Are you sure you don't want to meet separately on this issue? We could give it out undivided attention?"

"I think the next meeting will suffice."

"Yes, sir." Katherine gathered her papers into her briefcase and sat back down in her chair. She'd never felt so much hostility in all her life.

The hostility didn't stop at the doors of the library. It continued into the parking lot and at home. She managed to stand tall against the withering glances as she returned to her car and left the library, but she wasn't so strong when she listened to her answering machine at home.

Katherine remembered the old saying that good news traveled fast, but bad news traveled faster. The blinking light on her answering machine indicated at least a dozen messages.

Most callers didn't bother to leave their names, but they all knew hers.

Spending the next thirty minutes listening to disparaging remarks about her personal self, her career choice, and her daughter, left Katherine gasping for breath. She hurried to the screen-in patio and threw the door open inhaling deeply of the damp air.

Why can't those people understand the importance of this teenager center? These teenagers are screaming for help and no one hears them.

They're not going to get away with it. I'm not going to let them beat me. I will continue to fight for this center for the teenagers in this town. At the next meeting I'll be more prepared. I'll have all my ducks in a row and quacking in unison.

Feeling better and more relieved, Katherine had almost forgotten about the harassing telephone calls. It wasn't until the ringing of the phone pulled her out of her reflection that left her nerves jangling in harmony.

Determined not to let the public leaders intimidate her, Katherine answered the phone.

"Mrs. Marshall?"

"Yes ..." Katherine hesitated, tensing up for a confrontation.

"I just wanted to let you know that I totally agree with your suggestion for a community center for teenagers."

"You do, how wonderful. I'm sorry, I didn't get your name." Katherine fell against the counter relieved that she wasn't going to argue about her idea.

"A friend."

Chapter Twenty-Four

"Mike!"

"What?"

"I've been calling you to come downstairs for the last ten minutes. Get down here."

Mike stomped down the stairs and threw himself in a chair in the living room.

"Don't forget your appointment with the court appointed counselor."

"Yeah, I know."

"I'm serious. You've missed the last couple of appointments. I got a phone call at work about it."

"Okay. I know."

"Fine. You know. You know. You always know. I'm late."

Mike didn't look up to watch his dad hurry from the house. Instead, he hit the remote control for the television. He surfed channels not really seeing the choices. After several minutes he threw the remote control against the far wall. The ashtray followed quickly behind.

જી≈

"Katherine?"

"Yes, Jennie?"

"You have a phone call."

"Pass it through." Katherine rolled her eyes. Ever since she'd started back at the office, Jennie had been acting like a mother hen.

"I'm not sure you want to take the call."

"Who is it, Jennie?" Just the touch of impatience tinged Katherine's question.

"Charles Beckett."

Katherine lost her focus. She stammered to Jennie to have Mr. Beckett hold and she'd be right there.

After taking several deep breaths and waving Jennie back to her desk, Katherine picked up the telephone receiver. "Yes, Mr. Beckett, what can I do for you?"

"Mrs. Marshall, thank you for taking my call. How are you?"

"How am I? Why are you interested, Mr. Beckett? I'd think you could care less." Katherine blanched at her audacity.

"Okay, I deserved that."

"Mr. Beckett, why don't you explain why you called."

"Gotcha. No small talk. I'm writing an article that you might be interested in."

"Why's that?"

"I've uncovered a dirty little secret."

Katherine swallowed before asking, "And why would that interest me?"

"It's your dirty little secret."

"Mr. Beckett, if you are going to take up my time with playing games, I'll just say good-bye right now."

"Okay, you're going to play it cool. I can respect that."

"Well, thank you for calling, Mr. Beckett. I can't say I enjoyed our conversation." Katherine readied herself to hang up on the despicable reporter.

"Mrs. Marshall, Katherine ... I've found your mother. She's terminally ill. I think this would make a great follow up story to the others where I let my readers know about the single mother who was too into her career to take care of her daughter now seems to be as equally negligent at taking care of her terminally ill mother."

"You print a word of that and I'll make you sorry you ever learned how to spell."

"Threats Mrs. Marshall? It's not quite your style is it?"

"Mr. Beckett. I've been as patient with you as I can be under these circumstances. If you print anything that reeks of libel I'll sue you so fast you'll be left typing up ... menus for the high school cafeteria." Katherine heard a whoop and a laugh from the direction of the lobby.

"Do you have a mother?"

"Yes."

"Is she ill?"

"Yes, but I don't see ..."

"Have you kept in touch with her?"

"Okay, Mr. Beckett. I'm well aware of the fine line between truth and libel and the ridiculous games you reporters play with words. But, mark my words. If you cross that line I'll be the first one to stomp you."

"Well, it was wonderful talking to you, Mrs. Marshall. I really didn't have to call you and let you know what I was working on but I thought you might like to know."

"You're all heart."

"Maggie, you wouldn't believe this guy!" Katherine sat sideways on the comfortable overstuffed sofa chair sipping an iced tea while she fumed.

"Sounds like he really got to you."

"Yes, he did. But I think I handled it quite well."

"By telling him he should wish he never learned to spell?"

"You might be right. I did get a little out of hand." Katherine swallowed a sip of her tea and chuckled. "But, I wish I could have seen his face when I told him he would be spending the rest of his writing career writing cafeteria menus for the high school."

"Katie, you sure do have a way with words."

"Well, in a way he inadvertently helped me make a decision I've been wavering on for a couple of weeks."

"Oh? What decision."

"I called mom today." Katherine let her words sink in. "Did you hear me?"

"Katie, mom told me before you called."

"Oh."

"But, I think it's great that you made the first move."

"She doesn't sound very well, Mags."

"She's sick, Katie. She has been for a long time. Her liver is about gone. Emphysema took a hold in her lungs. The doctors don't give her but a few more years at the most."

"God, I'm so sorry. I knew it was bad. I mean, you'd been keeping me up to date on Mom's health, but I never really thought about it until I talked to her. Mags, I am a horrible daughter!"

"Oh Katherine, you're not a horrible daughter. If you were, you wouldn't have called mom."

"Is there anything the doctors can do?"

"No, just keep her comfortable and ease her pain toward the end."

"Mags, do you think mom would want to come here and stay? The weather is warmer, it could help a little, couldn't it?"

"Katie, I think mom would love to do that, but give her a little time, okay?"

"Sure, I understand. It must be quite a shock after so many years to hear from me again. Taking her from the only home she's been in nearly all her adult life and moving in with someone who is practically a stranger shouldn't be an impulsive decision."

"No, not really. But, I think she'll want to eventually. I mean, my home wouldn't be right for her, not with all the kids and grandkids running around. But, yours would be the best environment, especially with that warm air. I can just see mom sitting out on your patio next to the pool watching the squirrels play in the yard and the hummingbirds flit about the feeder."

"I know it's a little impulsive, but I am turning over a new leaf, Mags."

"You sure are, Lordy be girl, you're taking on the whole city council for this new project."

"It's important to me. But, more importantly, it's for the teenagers in this community."

"You sure you're not ... well, I mean ..."

"You mean am I trying to make amends to Anna?"

"Well, yes."

"Maybe, but is that so bad?"

"No, you're right. It's a good thing you're doing, and in the name of your daughter is even better."

"Thanks."

"Those kids are darn lucky to have someone like you to look after them."

"It's so sad, Mags. It really is. The kids at the school just seem so lost at times. They really need accurate information. They need someone to listen to them. They need someone to care about them."

"I think you'll be just the right person to give them all of that and more. I have faith in you, little sister."

"I wish there were more like you on the city council."

"They'll see the light. I'm sure of it. How can they not?"

"Well, if Mr. Charles Beckett keeps up with this shenanigans, it's going to be easy for them to say no."

"Well, he can't keep this up forever. Stand your ground."

"I will. I'm determined to see this through."

"Then you'll succeed. I'm sure of it. Oh, there goes the grandbaby. She's such a little doll baby, I could just eat her up."

"Are you babysitting tonight?"

"Yes, the kids haven't had a night to themselves since this little angel was born, so I volunteered to take the kids."

"I think that's wonderful. You better go. Sounds like she's being quite insistent."

"Yep, and Hank just sits there and looks lost, just like he did when the kids were babies. Some things never change."

Katherine sat and sipped her tea after she hung up with her sister. Some things never change. That may be so for some people, but not for her. She will change. She had changed. *I'm not going to take no for an answer. I'm going to make the city see how important this teen center is and they're going to accept it and build it. And, Mr. Charles Beckett can just take his pen and stuff it where the sun doesn't shine!*

Chapter Twenty-Five

Charles Beckett printed out his latest column for review. It was 2 am. His passion for satire and exposé hadn't disappointed him. Finishing a great column always made him hungry. Hungry and thirsty. He wandered into the kitchen to find a snack.

He tossed the printed papers onto the counter and opened the refrigerator. A groan sounded from a corner of the breakfast nook. "Turn off the light."

"Mike?"

"Yeah. Turn off the light." Mike's voice was muffled as he buried his face into his folded arms.

"What are you doing up? Did you just get home?"

"What do you care?"

"Don't talk to me like that. I'm still your father." Charles Beckett popped the top of a beer.

"Yeah. Right. Like that's ever made a difference."

"Mike? How can you say that?" He piled bologna and cheese onto bread and slathered mustard atop the feast. "I've raised you on my own, without the help of your so-called mother. We've been partners, you and I. It's been us against the world." Charles Beckett sat next to his son at the table. "We're buds."

"We're not buds."

"We're friends, aren't we?"

"I don't really feel like talking right now. I'm tired." Mike started to get up from the table.

"Oh, sit. Have a beer with your old man." Charles Beckett opened the refrigerator and removed another beer. He slid it across the table to his son.

Mike opened the beer and drank it quickly. He belched then covered his mouth with his hand. "Sorry."

"No need to apologize. We're bachelors, living in a bachelor pad."

Charles Beckett retrieved his printed column and concentrated on reviewing it with the limited glow from the small light over the table.

"Dad ..." Mike contemplated his father's bent head.

"Hmmm ..." Charles Beckett didn't look up from the paper.

"Never mind." Mike pulled the first printed page toward him. Bored, he half-read it while sipping his beer.

Charles Beckett made a few notations while he read. He slid the pencil back behind his ear and stretched his arms above his head while yawning.

"What is this?" Mike took the rest of the papers and spread them out in front of him.

"My column for the newspaper. What do you think?"

Mike kept his facial expressions neutral. "I dunno."

"Go on, tell me what you really think."

Mike squirmed in his chair. He didn't look up to meet his father's eyes. "Kinda harsh, I guess."

"Harsh?"

"Yeah."

"Okay, Mr. Critic." Charles Beckett leaned back in his chair. "What's so harsh about it?"

"How can you say all this stuff? What did this lady ever do to you? God, you even got my friends talking about it. I know what's really going on."

"Okay, you think you know it all, tell me what's really going on?"

"You're just pissed about mom. She really did a number on you, didn't she?"

"You don't know what you're talking about."

"Do you always have to be like that? Can't anyone else have an opinion other than your own?"

"So, Mr. High School Graduate, what would you write? Huh?" Charles Beckett snatched the papers from his son's hands. "You wouldn't, of course."

Mike found a burst of anger that erupted from his body through his voice. "That's right!" He flung himself out of his chair so hard that it tipped over behind him. "No one is better than you, right? Right!" Mike felt the rage surge through him. "You think that whatever you say or write, people will fall all over themselves to lay at your feet. You're not God, dad." Mike saw the look of surprise in his father's face. "Yeah, that's right. News flash. Charles Beckett is not God. You don't always have to have the last word. You don't always have to cast judgment."

"What in the hell has gotten into you?"

"Can't you just leave it alone? Let it go!"

"Let what go?"

"You just don't understand."

"Then why don't you explain it to me."

"Anna." Mike picked up the fallen chair and slumped down onto its seat. "My girlfriend is dead, dad. Dead."

"It was an accident. It could have happened to anyone."

"I don't think so, dad."

"What are you talking about?"

"I loved her. She was my life." Mike's chin dropped lower into his chest.

"Mike, Mike, Mike. There'll be other girls. Lots of girls. You're young. You have lots of time to fall in love."

Mike shook his head back and forth. "You just don't get it." He looked up at his dad. "I loved her. I'm nothing without her."

"Mike, don't say that. You have your whole life ahead of you. Don't throw it away on an accident that could have happened to anyone."

"That's just it!" Mike's rage burst forth again. "It didn't happen to just anyone. It happened to Anna. Anna!" Dejected with an overwhelming sense of fatigue, Mike dragged himself out of his chair and stood before his father. "I'm tired. I'm going to bed."

"Good idea. Get some sleep. You'll feel better in the morning."

"Yeah. Right."

"Oh, c'mon, Mike. The rest of the city has put the accident behind them, so can you."

"I'll never forget her, dad. Ever." Mike threw his empty beer can toward the garbage can and ran upstairs.

Charles Beckett bolted straight up in bed. He glanced at the clock. 6:45 am. What had wakened him?

Another scream pierced the shadows. Charles threw the covers back and raced down the hall to his son's bedroom door.

Charles listened but didn't hear any response. He pushed open the door and peered into the darkness.

"Mike?" Charles whispered. He stepped into his son's room. He nearly gagged at the sour offensive odor. Dirty clothes, stale cigarette smoke, and something he didn't want to identify hung in the humid, stuffy room. He held a hand to his nose as he stumbled his way over pizza boxes, beer cans, and piles of clothes.

The morning light filtered through the partially closed blinds. Charles could make out Mike's tossing form on the bed. His son kicked his legs and flung his arm over his head. He moaned as if in pain.

"Mike, you're dreaming." Charles touched his son lightly on the shoulder.

Mike shook off his touch. "Lemme go. I gotta save her."

"Hey, Mike. Wake up. You're having a nightmare." Charles nudged his son harder.

"Anna!"

Charles jumped, startled by his son's scream. He grabbed him by the shoulders and awkwardly held him in his arms. "Mike, shhhh ... Mike, it's okay. You're just having a bad dream." He patted his son's sweaty back. He felt Mike's chest heave as he gulped for air.

"Hey, it's all right. You were having a nightmare. I came in to see how you were." He looked over at his son. Shocked, he realized they were the same height. When was the last time he could see over the top of his son's head? Charles couldn't answer the question. Hesitating, unsure of what he should do next, he reached out to his son. "Do you remember anything of your nightmare?"

"No." Embarrassed, Mike answered fast, then pushed himself back from his father. "Thanks," he mumbled. "I'll be okay." He lay back down on his pillow. "I'm tired."

"Well, all right then. You get some sleep. Good night."

Through half-closed eyes, Mike watched his father turn and leave. As soon as the door shut behind him, Mike pushed his pillow higher against the headboard and sat up.

He fumbled for his cigarettes and lighter among the empty packs, cellophane, and empty soda and beer cans on his nightstand. Finding one, he lit it quickly and sucked hard.

He wasn't bothered by the lie he told his father. Of course he remembered his dream. He'd been having the same kind of dreams for the last week. Every night Anna's face haunted him.

At first, he thought it was because he missed her so much. But, a couple of nights ago, she spoke to him. She asked him why he killed her if he loved her so much?

Flashes of memory like photographs flipped through his mind. Tonight was the worst. *I remember*, he thought. *I remember the whole stinking night.*

That night was supposed to be their night; their special night. They'd graduated high school. They were on top of the world. Nothing could stop them from being together, forever. At least, to Mike.

But, Mike knew deep inside that something was different. Anna was different. She stood up to him more. She wasn't going along with all of his plans.

"C'mon Anna, just say yes, okay?" Mike hung onto the side of the pool with one hand and plucked the sucker out of his mouth with the other.

"No, Mike. I can't. I'm going to school in California." Anna pushed Mike back a bit. She was feeling claustrophobic with him so close. Her stomach churned. She tugged on Mike's hand holding the sucker, positioning it toward her mouth. Maybe the cherry sucker would settle the sloshing alcohol in her stomach.

"Why can't you go to a school here in Florida, or at least on the east coast?"

"I was accepted by the college in California, that's why." Anna rubbed the right side of her jaw. She clenched and unclenched it trying to ease the ache. She put her arms around Mike's shoulders to keep from sinking.

Mike pouted. His lower lip puffed out. He gave Anna his best hang-dog look. She never could resist his puppy-dog face.

"Mike, don't do that. I'm not changing my mind."

Desperate, Mike grabbed Anna's shoulders. His fingers dug deep into her flesh.

"Dammit, Anna. Marry me!"

"No. Now, let me go. My skin's getting all pruned." Anna squirmed and shoved her wrinkled hand in Mike's face. The bracelet that Mike had given her flashed and twinkled.

Enraged, Mike slapped Anna's hand away. Anger pulsed through his body. He lost control. He slapped her face and then grabbed her head and held it beneath the water. He kept his back to the rest of the pool not wanting the others to see what he was doing.

Mike crushed out his cigarette and lay back on the bed. He had killed the only person who he truly loved. Tears filled his eyes. He held his pillow over his face to muffle the sobs.

Chapter Twenty-Six

Charles Beckett pulled himself from a deep sleep to turn off the alarm. Showered and shaved, dressed only in a pair of khaki slacks, he rapped on Mike's door as he passed it on his way downstairs. "Yo, Mike. Time to get up."

In the kitchen, he poured himself a cup of coffee from the automatic coffee maker. "Best damn purchase I ever made," he mumbled to himself as he sipped carefully of the hot liquid.

Stepping outside in his bare feet to pick up the morning paper, he nearly choked on the humidity. Glancing at the dark clouds whirling above, he estimated it would probably rain before he got to the office.

A quick check of the clock told him that Mike was going to be late for his counselor if he didn't hurry. "Mike," he shouted from the bottom of the stairs. "Get up!"

Not hearing a response, Charles stomped up the stairs and pounded on Mike's door. The door opened and his bleary-eyed son peered from behind it. "What?"

"Get up. You have an appointment this morning."

"I don't feel good."

"You sick?"

"Yeah. Sick." Mike went to close the door.

"Wait, let me check your head." Charles put a hand on his son's forehead then wiped his hand on the side of his pant leg.

"Knock it off."

"Well, you're a little cool and clammy." Charles patted his son on the shoulder. "Call and reschedule if you're sick. Otherwise, get there, got it?"

"Yeah." Mike closed the door before his dad could say anything else.

Charles managed to make it through the day with only two people bold enough to tell him about Katherine Marshall's accomplishments with the volunteer program at the high school. According to one of his sources, she'd apparently succeeded in helping several students at the school. Her free parenting group sessions were getting favorable reviews.

He'd even heard that there were supporters for her teen center proposal. She'd managed to get the mayor to consider her proposal if she could gather more than 50 percent of the voters' signatures. A snitch in the mayor's office told him that she was well on her way.

He'd spent most of the day reading letters from angry citizens telling him to lay off Katherine Marshall and move on to a new subject. Some of the letters made their point with colorful language. An anonymous sender included a picture of a dead horse.

Shuffling papers into a drawer, Charles picked up his briefcase and headed out of his office. He'd had enough for the day. His head hurt and he needed a beer.

Walking through the parking lot to his car, his cell phone rang.

"Hello?"

"Mr. Beckett?"

"Yes."

"Mr. Beckett, this is Sylvia from the Bridgeway Behavioral Center. Your son, Mike had an appointment today."

"Didn't he keep it?"

"No, that's what I'm calling you about."

"He did say something about being sick this morning. Can he reschedule?"

"Mr. Beckett. Mike hasn't kept the last two appointments. Today makes three he's missed."

"That can't be. He told me ... he went."

"Mr. Beckett. Your son is violating a court order by not attending these sessions. All we can do is report to the judge and let them take it from there."

"I understand. Thank you."

The three beers he'd had before he got home did nothing to help his headache. He popped open another one while he headed upstairs to see Mike. Stopping in front of his son's bedroom door, he took a long swallow before knocking.

"Mike?"

No answer.

"Mike!" Charles pounded on the door.

Still no answer.

Charles wriggled the doorknob to see if the door was locked. It opened with a twist of his wrist. He stepped inside from the light of the hall into the gloom of the darkened room. His senses were immediately assaulted with odors even more obnoxious than the night before. Sour sweat and flat beer wafted over him. "Mike, are you in here?"

He stepped carefully remembering the piles of dirty clothes, pizza boxes, fast food bags, and cans. Even being careful he still managed to step on an old pizza crust that when broke sounded like it was fossilized.

Stepping over the trashcan near the bed, he almost toppled it with his foot. Catching it before it fell, he gagged as the odor of vomit hit his nose. He backed away quickly, nearly spilling his beer as he hurried to the hall to get a breath of fresh air.

Charles pulled a washcloth out of the linen closet and held it over his nose before he walked back into his son's room. "Mike? Are you all right?" He shook his son's shoulder trying to waken him.

"What?" Groggy, Mike opened one eye.

"Mike, are you sick?"

"Yeah." Mike rolled over on his back.

Charles stepped back. Mike's body odor and the unpleasant smell of stale beer clung to the boy. He'd had an understanding with Mike. He could drink, as long as he was at home, and if he didn't overdo it. This was more than he could handle.

"You're drunk."

Mike tried to lift his head. He couldn't. He opened his eyes, but "So" was all he could say before closing his eyes again.

Hurrying out of his son's room, Charles knew that Mike was in no condition to listen to a lecture. *I'm not really in the mood to deliver one, either. What is the matter with that kid? Maybe he's rebelling against something. I'll have to figure it out and see how I can help him.*

Charles Beckett wandered into his office and sat at his desk. He turned on his computer and logged onto the Internet. He'd surf a few sites and see if he could find some answers about teenagers and alcohol.

≈≈

Katherine couldn't believe her ears. The Friends of Bridgeway Library group had asked her to attend their meeting and discuss how to meet the local teenagers' needs. This was just the leverage she needed to help sway the city council.

She used her cell phone to call Jennie on her way to the library. "Jennie, try and reschedule my appointments for the rest of the day. I'm heading over to the library to talk about the teen programs."

"Hey, that's great! Your three-thirty called and cancelled so all I have to do is contact your five o'clock."

"Thanks, Jen. Keep your fingers crossed that this meeting goes well."

"Will do, give 'em hell."

Katherine smiled as she pressed the end button to disconnect her call. Smiling didn't come as easy to her as it used to, but she was finding more to smile about. Beckett's newspaper column seemed to have found another target, she was getting more support for the teen center, and her life didn't seem so dismal.

She planned on getting to the library early so she could check out a couple of books she wanted to pick up for her next parent's meeting.

Nose in a book, she turned the corner at the end of a bookshelf and ran into someone kneeling down.

"Oh, excuse me. I'm sorry. I wasn't watching ..." Katherine's apology faded away when she realized who she had tripped over.

Charles Beckett stood to face the person who almost fell over him. "No problem, my fault." He stopped talking, but his mouth didn't close. "Oh."

"Hello, Mr. Beckett." Katherine looked over her shoulder for the nearest exit. It was across the room.

"Mrs. Marshall." Charles Beckett paused for a moment. Then on impulse, said, "Don't worry, I don't bite."

Suspicious, Katherine asked him what he was doing at the library.

"Research." Beckett responded.

A quick glance told Katherine that the books he was looking at were on teenager behavior. Was he there to ruin her chance with the library group? Her chin came up and her back stiffened, "Why?"

He didn't meet her eyes. "Personal reasons."

"Oh." Katherine wondered if he was telling the truth. The next question was asked before Katherine thought about what she was saying. "Is there anything I can do?"

"You?" Charles Beckett asked. "You are offering to help me after I ..." He left the sentence drag out and didn't finish it aloud.

"Is it Mike?" Katherine asked in a quiet voice.

Charles took a deep breath and blew it out in a sigh. "Yeah. I just can't seem to reach him." Unable to stop them, the rest of the words tumbled out of his mouth in a rush to be heard. "Last week I came home and he was drunk. Passed out drunk in his room. I've been trying all the suggestions from the Internet. I've yelled at him. I took all the beer out of the house. I tried talking to him. I even tried making a deal with him that if he quit drinking I would too. Nothing worked. He just sits in his room all day and ignores me. He's even ignoring his friends. He doesn't go anywhere, he doesn't want to see anyone."

"Has he said anything to you? Anything at all?"

"Well, he said that he missed, umm ... that Anna's death hit him really hard."

Katherine bit her lip. "I guess it's understandable. He's grieving."

"Yeah, maybe you're right. I don't know what to do. A couple of Internet sites recommended some books so I came here to pick them up." He motioned to the pile of books on the floor.

"I'm here for sort of the same reason." Katherine shifted the books in her right arm to the left. "I'm picking up books for my parenting session. Hey, wait a minute. Why don't you come to our next meeting?

You may not find all the answers you're looking for but you could commiserate with some other parents who'll know what you're going through. It'll keep you from feeling all alone." Katherine smiled.

Charles Beckett watched the smile play across Katherine Marshall's lips. It didn't look like she smiled much anymore. His stomach twisted into a knot realizing that he was probably one of the main reasons why. Her offer of parenting classes must have cost her a lot. "Maybe."

He watched the smile fade away. "Yeah, sure. I understand."

"Wait." He couldn't believe he was going to say this, "I don't really want the whole town to know about Mike and, well ... I don't know ... can you understand?"

"Yeah, sure, I understand." Katherine shifted the books again and turned to go.

"But, I wouldn't mind talking to you about it, just us, no group session." Charles bent and picked up the books he wanted to read and hurried to catch up with Katherine.

"You don't have to pretend, Mr. Beckett."

"I'm not. I would really like to talk to you about this."

Katherine whirled around. "All right. If you're serious about this, meet me at the coffee shop next door in two hours."

"Two hours?"

"Right. I have a meeting here at the library. I'll meet you next door when I'm through." She looked as if she didn't believe he'd accept.

Charles nodded before he spoke. "All right. Meet you there."

The librarian scanned Katherine's card and slid the return date cards in the jacket pocket. Charles watched her cock her head as he listened to their conversation. He pushed his card and books toward her and closed his mouth. He wasn't going to give her any more information to gossip with to her friends.

He walked with Katherine to the meeting room and as he left said, "I'll be next door waiting."

Exactly two hours later, Katherine opened the coffee shop door. The bells hanging on the inside jangled her entrance. She searched the booths and found Mike's father sitting at the back of the small shop in the booth furthest from the door and cash register.

She caught his attention and half-raised her arm to wave. She lowered it after realizing she wasn't here to meet a friend for coffee.

Charles lifted his head when he heard the bells jingle. To be totally honest with himself, he'd lifted his head each time the door opened, although he knew it couldn't possibly be her. She'd said two hours, and if his most recent impressions of Katherine Marshall were correct, she wouldn't show for two hours. If the shoe were on the other foot, he'd probably leave her waiting longer. He mentally kicked himself for acting like such an idiot.

She put her raincoat over the back of the seat and sat across from him. Tiny drops of rain were caught in her hair and on her eye-lashes. She pulled a few napkins from the metal holder on the table and dabbed at her hair and face.

She's pretty he thought to himself then immediately told himself to snap out of it.

"How'd the meeting go?" He asked, hoping to squelch the voice inside.

"It went well." Katherine finished wiping the rain from her face and played with the napkin while she talked. "Much better than I could have ever imagined. The library is going to put together a teen group that will choose projects that will interest teenagers. Everything from book reviews, to poetry readings, to a battle of the bands contest."

"Sounds good."

"It is, it really is. Teenagers aren't inherently bad. They just get bored easily. They need some structure, some activities that they can get involved in without looking 'uncool.'"

Charles laughed. "Uncool?"

The waitress arrived before they could say anything else. Katherine ordered a cup of coffee and Charles asked for a refill.

They didn't speak again until Katherine was sipping from her cup.

Charles didn't know how to broach the subject. Helpless, he looked at Katherine, hoping she would read the humiliation on his face and understand.

Katherine realized Charles Beckett was embarrassed about his situation. She slipped into therapist mode and coaxed him from his shell.

"So, tell me about Mike."

Charles straightened from his slouch and looked down at the table. "He's been down for awhile, I guess. At first I brushed it off as typical reaction after graduation. Not really knowing what to do with himself. Then, well ..." He looked up into Katherine's face.

She kept her face neutral, but smiled a little to encourage him. Katherine knew that he needed to cover some awkward ground, espe-cially since Mike had been Anna's boyfriend. She motioned him to go on.

"Well, I guess Anna's death hit him pretty hard. But, he didn't really get a chance to absorb it all, what with the trial and all."

Katherine nodded.

"Then, when he was acquitted, well he was happy, I thought. He was hanging out with his friends, going to the beach, like he used to. But, then, he stopped going out with his friends. Then he stopped seeing them when they'd stop by. He hasn't taken a phone call in I don't know how long. He just stays in his room, smoking and drink-ing."

"Are you providing him with the beer?"

Charles squirmed in his seat. "I was, at first. But, not anymore. I took it all out of the house. I don't even drink at home anymore."

"Have you tried talking to him."

"Yeah." Charles fiddled with the spoon on the table. "Now he doesn't even let me in his room anymore. He keeps it locked. I have to practically camp out in the hall just to catch him when he makes a trip to the bathroom." Charles flipped the spoon upside down. "Which isn't very often, that's for sure. I don't even know when was the last time he took a shower."

"Does he have a telephone in his room?"

"He did. Not anymore. He ripped it out of the wall and threw it down the hall one day last week when I told him he had a phone call." Charles shifted in his seat. He looked like he had something more to say. "Look, Mrs. Marshall, I don't think this is going to work. I mean, I ripped you pretty hard in the newspaper. Mostly, I was doing my job, but some of it was personal."

Katherine shrugged her shoulders. She let Charles Beckett make his apology. She deserved it and wanted to hear it. A part of her still held a grudge against this man who made her days such a living hell through the most despondent time of her life.

Katherine waited for the human quality she sensed in Charles Beckett to reach out to her.

"Unfortunately, I let my personal issues take over my judgment." He dropped his head into his hands and ran his fingers through his hair. "God, this is so hard."

Katherine didn't want to distract him from his confession or apology or whatever he was trying to do, so she kept still and waited.

Charles looked up. "I didn't mean to hurt you, not really. I was mostly angry at your profession—counselors, therapists, you know."

Katherine nodded, hoping she could keep him talking.

"I'm not doing this very well. Let me back up a bit. Mike's mother left ... well, we were divorced when Mike was twelve, no thirteen, no he was twelve, because he was still in middle school. Anyway, it was rough on him. His mother and I went to marriage counseling for months."

Katherine caught the inflection in his voice when he mentioned marriage counseling. She sipped her coffee. "I see," she said.

"No, I don't think you do. It wasn't just that the counseling didn't work. Megan, she made a decision that affected our entire life. Mine and Mike's."

"Do you want to tell me about that decision?"

"Maybe. Yes. Look, Mrs. Marshall—"

"Wait, before we go any further, can we cut out the Mrs. And Mr. Stuff? We're just two people talking, okay? Call me Katherine, please."

"Thank you. I'm Charles. Charlie to my friends."

Katherine nodded. She motioned to the waitress to refill their cups before asking Charles to continue.

"Mike had a hard time with the counseling sessions. We'd have family sessions where Megan, Mike, and I would have to sit and talk about what was happening with our family situation. Mike suffered a lot in those sessions. He didn't understand what was happening between his mother and me. Shit. I didn't understand what was happening with his mother and me. I still don't. I guess that's why I carry such a huge chip when it comes to therapists."

"It must have been difficult for him, especially having to go through puberty at the same time. Do you think that he's still holding back feelings from your divorce?"

"It's possible. He even said something to that effect the other night. I guess I've been so focused on my own vendetta that I didn't take into consideration what was happening to him."

"It sounds like you have some very strong feelings for therapy. Are you upset because you invested so much time and energy into your marriage with therapy and it didn't work out?"

"Not really. I'm more upset at therapists in general, I think. I thought that Megan and I were there to work out our differences. But, only a few sessions into the counseling and Megan was asking for separate sessions. So, I agreed. I thought that she might have some personal issues to deal with. If so, I wanted her to resolve them. Maybe she'd figure them out and we'd be a family again. It didn't happen that way."

"What happened?"

"We'd been in counseling for a few months when Megan asked me to meet her at a restaurant down by the beach for lunch. She said she wanted to talk. Over some friggin' conch fritters she tells me she's leaving me; leaving us, Mike and me."

"I'm sorry. I'm sure you must have been very hurt and felt deceived?"

"That ain't the half of it. She tells me that she's discovered ..." Charles held up his hands to imitate quotes. "Discovered that she was a lesbian."

Katherine almost choked on the mouthful of coffee.

"Yeah, I see it hit you about like it hit me." Charles handed her a napkin to wipe up the puddle of coffee.

"I'm sorry. I guess I just wasn't expecting this."

"It's okay. I wasn't either ..." he half smiled a crooked grin.

"So she left, just like that?"

"Yep. Just like that. She went home, packed up her stuff and told me to file for divorce, that she wouldn't contest it."

"What about Mike? How'd he take it?"

"At first, we told him we were separating, just to see if we could work things out by ourselves, that we needed some time apart. But, he wasn't buying it. I think he knew all along that we would end up getting a divorce."

"Did he ever find out about his mother?"

"Yeah. That's the worst part. His mother would pick him up for visitation, and she'd spend time with him and her new partner. He came home from the first time he met her and swore he'd never see his mother again. And he hasn't. I haven't forced him and he's never asked to see her or even talk to her on the telephone."

"He couldn't handle her lifestyle change?"

"Something like that. Actually, he couldn't deal with the woman she chose as her partner." Charles looked away from the table and stared out the window. "It was our marriage counselor."

"Oh my God."

"Yeah." Thirsty, Charles took a long gulp of his coffee.

Chapter Twenty-Seven

On his drive back home, Charles Beckett reflected on his conversation with Katherine Marshall. He'd told her some extremely personal issues but didn't feel all that embarrassed about it. She didn't act condescending toward him, for that he was grateful. If she had, he'd probably be dictating a scathing column into his tape recorder. As it was, he felt something close to remorse for the horrible way he'd treated her these past few months.

She'd been very forgiving for his conduct. He'd apologized over and over for taking his anger and hurt out on her.

She had peaked his interested when she described the teen center she wanted the city to build. Her intentions were good. She had a solid understanding of the needs of the teens and the benefits to the community. Why he didn't see it before was understandable. He'd been so interested in bombarding the news with his personal attacks on therapists that he didn't see reality. Reality was his son's problem with alcohol. Alcohol and probably drugs.

When he left, he suggested to Katherine Marshall that she contact a friend of his at Community Relations. He still remembered the look of surprise on her face at his offer.

Her offer for future talks sure surprised him. His first reaction was pleasant. Now, he wondered about his intentions. Was he looking forward to seeing her as a therapist or a friend?

He was eager to get home and maybe try the suggestions she offered to help communicate with Mike. He hoped that he and Mike could at least get back to the way they were, and maybe even try a few sessions with the therapist that Katherine had suggested. He appreciated her grasp of the sensitivity of the issues and not willing to handle the behavioral therapy herself. That spoke volumes to him about her professionalism.

Charles parked his car in the garage and sat for a few minutes to collect his thoughts. He had called the house on his way home, but didn't really expect Mike to answer. He'd refused to answer the phone or even talk to anyone who called. He left a message on the answering machine letting Mike know he would be home shortly and wanted to talk to him.

His mood lifted, Charles whistled a nonsense tune while putting his briefcase away and trotting up the stairs. He rapped 'shave and a haircut' on Mike's door while a smile found its way to his face. It wasn't until he knocked again that he noticed an odd smell seeping from beneath the door. His nose wrinkled in distaste. He'd steeled himself for the usual sour, stale smells of Mike's room, but this was decidedly different; sweet, but disgusting at the same time.

Charles tried the doorknob. It turned easily in his hand. He opened the door slowly and stepped into the darkened room. Stepping carefully, he made his way to Mike's bed. His son lay on his side, his face toward the door. Charles touched his shoulder to gently waken him. Instead of encountering the cotton fabric of his son's t-shirt, his fingers instead sank into thick fluid. Charles backed up. He fumbled for the light switch.

With the light on, Charles could see that his son lay in a thick red, gray pool of blood, brain tissue, and body fluids. The .22 caliber handgun that he kept in his nightstand was in his son's lifeless hand.

"Oh, God ... no ... no ... no ..." Charles knelt down next to the bed and cradled his son's body in his arms.

The rest of the evening went by in a blur for Charles. He called 911 and soon the house was filled with Emergency Medical Technicians, police officers, and various police and emergency personnel. Charles watched as the coroner's technicians arrived to put Mike into a black body bag and carry him downstairs to their vehicle. He kept his composure while curious neighbors looked on behind the police barricade but back inside the house the tears fell freely.

He answered numerous questions while other EMT and police officers stood around carrying on low conversations in bored tones.

Charles felt his grip on civility loosen, as he had to answer the same questions repeatedly. Detective Murphy appeared on the scene and after being briefed by the officers on duty turned to Charles.

"Did you ever suspect that your son might be suicidal?"

"No."

Did you suspect he had a drug problem?"

"No, not really."

"Did you suspect he had an alcohol problem?"

"Yes."

"Was he seeing a counselor?"

"Yes, one appointed by the court. I'll get you the number." Charles disappeared into his office then returned with the counselor's name and number.

"Did he have a girlfriend?"

"No, Yes. I mean no, she died of an accidental drowning a few months ago."

"The Marshall girl?" Detective Murphy eyed Charles Beckett with a wary look. It hadn't been that long ago he was in this very same house questioning the boy about the Marshall girl's death.

"Yeah, that's the one."

"Did your son have any enemies? Did he owe anyone money?"

"Not that I know of. He'd been hanging out in his room mostly the last week or so. He'd get a few phone calls, but he never took them."

"What about—" the detective stopped when another police officer touched his shoulder and gave him a piece of paper. He read it then nodded to the police officer signaling that he'd take care of it.

"Mr. Beckett ..."

"What, what is it? Is it about Mike?" Charles saw the officer exchange glances with Detective Murphy.

"Maybe you should read this. It looks like Mike left you a note."

Charles' hand shook as he reached for the piece of paper with his son's handwriting. He sat at the kitchen table while he read his son's last words.

Dear Dad,

I'm sorry for putting you through this, but I don't have any other choice. I killed Anna. I know that now. I remember what happened that awful night. I asked her to marry me but she said no. I slapped her and I held her head under the water until she drowned. I hate myself for what I did. I can't go on living while the only person whom I ever loved and who loved me is dead.

I'm sorry.

Your son, Mike.

Charles folded his arms across the table and lay his head down. Tears streamed down his face. The police officers turned their backs to give him as much privacy as they could.

Detective Murphy patted Beckett's shoulder and asked, "Is there anyone I can call for you?"

Without even thinking the first words out of Beckett's mouth were, "Katherine Marshall."

He sat up quickly when he realized what he said.

Detective Murphy's jaw dropped. He'd thought there was nothing left in the world that could surprise him. He looked at Beckett with a strange confusion.

Beckett didn't look back. He only said, "No, wait. I'll call her myself."

Chapter Twenty-Eight

Restless after the police and other official personnel left, Charles Beckett wandered the rooms downstairs, but refused to take one step up to the second floor.

He'd answered questions until he was blue in the face and thought he would fall over from fatigue. Now, he couldn't sit still. He grabbed his keys and headed for the garage.

He avoided acknowledging his destination until he sat in the driveway with his engine idling. Charles hesitated now that he was actually there. Putting the car in reverse, he prepared to back out of the driveway when the front porch light turned on.

Gathering his reserve, he knocked on the front door.

"Charles, I'm surprised to see you here. Is everything okay?"

"Hello Katherine, May I come in?"

"Sure, come in. Can I get you anything?" Katherine showed Charles into the living room.

"No, yes ... do you have any beer? No, wait, just some coffee." Charles sank into the cushions of the sofa.

Katherine busied herself by preparing a tray for the coffee. While she waited for the coffee to drip in the glass pot she wondered why Charles Beckett showed up on her doorstep this late.

Carrying the tray into the living room she caught a glimpse of the man sitting on her sofa. His eyes drooped. His shoulders slumped.

"Here we go. Fresh coffee."

Charles waited as Katherine poured him a cup. He wrapped his hands around the ceramic cup. When did his hands get so cold?

Katherine waited. She knew he had something to say and it would come in its own time.

Charles held his cup in both hands then looked at the one person who he thought could possibly understand what had happened to him. "Katherine, Mike killed ... committed suicide tonight."

"Oh, Charles. I'm so sorry." Katherine laid a hand on his trembling arm.

Charles tried to put the coffee cup on the low table in front of him, but he couldn't see it for the tears in his eyes.

"Here, let me take that for you." Katherine rescued the tilting cup from his unresisting hands and placed it on the tray.

"It was a horrifying sight." Charles drew a deep breath. He wiped his face with the back of his hand. "I came home ready to talk to him about my breakthrough and I went upstairs ..."

"You don't have to talk about it right now, if it's too difficult. I understand."

"I know you do. That's why I want to talk about it." Charles grabbed her hand. "I need to tell you this."

"All right." Katherine left her hand in his.

He turned to face Katherine. "Mike shot himself with my gun. I ... I never got to tell him I was sorry for putting him through such a horrible divorce."

"I understand your feelings of guilt, but don't blame yourself. This wasn't your fault."

Charles clasped Katherine's hand between his. "Katherine, he left a note. Oh, God. I don't know how to tell you this. But I want you to hear it from me, rather than anyone else."

A shiver raced through Katherine's body. No longer did she feel that Charles ended up on her doorstep just for someone to talk to. Somehow, Mike's suicide meant something to her. She waited for him to continue.

"Mike confessed in his note that he ... Katherine, please forgive me ... he said that he kil—was responsible for Anna's death."

"What?" Katherine removed her hand from Charles' and pressed the palms against her cheeks.

"I'm sorry. I am so sorry."

"He killed Anna?"

"Apparently, he asked her to marry him that night, but she said no. He ... he was hurt and angry." Charles coughed to clear his throat. How could he tell her that his son held her daughter's head under water until she drowned? "I don't know what to say or do to make this any easier. I don't want to make excuses for him. It won't make it go away. Mike mentioned in his letter that he didn't remember until just recently what happened that night."

A loud buzzing in Katherine's head made his words sound far away. Anna didn't drown. Anna was killed. Anna's killer was dead. What did that mean to her? None of it brought Anna back. Anna was still dead. Her grief rose like bile in the back of her throat. "What in the world could you possibly have been thinking?"

"I guess I wasn't."

Katherine leapt to her feet and paced the room. She pushed a lock of hair that fell in front of her eyes with shaky fingers. Her voice shook as well as she exploded. "Your son ... my daughter ... their lives cut so short ..."

"I know. I know."

"I can't deal with this." She picked up her coffee cup from the table and drained its contents. "This can't be happening." In a swift move, she flung the cup across the room toward the fireplace. The cup shattered against the rock face.

"Christ!" Charles yelled and jumped to his feet.

"I want to scream!"

"Then do it. Scream. Yell. Throw something else."

Sinking into a sofa chair, tired and anger spent, Katherine looked over at Charles. "When will this nightmare end?"

"If it was within my power I would make it all different."

"Charles, I'm sorry, here I am wallowing in my own self-pity and you are suffering too."

"You have every right."

"No, I'm sorry. You just lost your son tonight. I'm so insensitive." Katherine moved from the chair to sit next to Charles on the sofa. She started to pour another cup of coffee and realized she didn't have a cup. A sob burst from her throat.

"I can't do this ... I can't go through this again."

"I know. I'm so sorry. If I could take it all back, I'd do it in a heartbeat." Charles sank back into the sofa. Elbows on knees he held his head in his hands. "I take full responsibility for this. I'll do whatever you want. I'll do whatever I can to make this up to you."

"It wasn't you. Please, stop. It's self-defeating. You know what it was, don't you?" Katherine called from the kitchen as she retrieved another cup.

Charles knelt in front of the fireplace and picked up ceramic shards. "No, what?"

"Those damn drugs." She walked back into the living room. "What are you doing?"

"I'm picking up the broken cup. I need something to do."

"I understand. Here, let me take those from you."

"No, sit down. Pour yourself a cup of coffee. I'm sure I can find my way from here to the kitchen trash and back."

"Thank you."

When he returned, Charles asked Katherine, "You were saying something about drugs?"

"I don't think you should take the blame for this. I think the true blame lies with the drugs and alcohol. It's impaired these kids. They've warped their mind with that garbage. It's becoming quite clear to me that the drugs are ruining these kids."

"You might have something there. I wouldn't have admitted it before, but I think you just might have something there."

"There's a lot of national programs that we can bring into this town. We aren't alone in this."

"But those kids aren't going to listen to a bunch of adults telling them that drugs are bad."

"You're right about that. But, it doesn't have to be adults telling the teenagers. It can be teenagers telling teenagers. They're more likely to listen to their peers than adults, anyway. And, there are organizations like the Teen Agency Council that prepare for just such situations. They are a network of social service agencies and community members that work to get teenagers involved by discouraging this kind of illegal behavior. It's been very successful in other cities. Believe it or not, there are teenagers who don't do drugs and don't drink and want to help others."

"No kidding?" Charles tried to smile.

"Very funny. But, yes, there are. I met quite a few while volunteering at the high school."

"I'd like to help, but, who'd listen to me, now?"

"You have a very powerful influence among this community. I think you'll be pleasantly surprised."

"Even after they find out that my son ... committed ... killed ... himself?"

"Charles Beckett, are you ashamed of your son?"

"Hell no, but ..."

"But what?"

"What kind of parent will they think I am, that my son did this to himself?"

"You did your best. We are all human. Not perfect, just human. Charles, I had the same doubts about myself when I found out that Anna was into illegal drugs and alcohol. I berated myself something terrible. I laid awake nights wondering if I had been a better mother would she still be alive today? Of course, it didn't help that I was faced with those doubts every time I read the newspaper ..." Katherine faced Charles.

"God, I was such an idiot. I'm sorry. I am so sorry. I wish I could take it all back."

"It's in the past. Charles, we have to put it behind us. It's not going to do either of us any good, or the memories of our children if we continue to fight. It's done and over with. We move on. We have to, for the sake of the other teenagers in this community. I refuse to let another day go by without trying to help."

"What can I do?"

"Don't let your son's death be for nothing. Honor his memory. Grieve for him, then vow to help others."

"I can't believe he's gone. If I hadn't seen it for myself, I wouldn't believe it. Why did he do that to himself? Why didn't he come to me?"

"Mike was distraught. He was living with a heavy burden. One that he didn't think he'd ever be able to overcome."

"That stupid gun. I should never have bought it. If only I didn't have it in the house."

"Don't blame yourself. The gun wasn't the reason Mike committed suicide. The gun was the facilitator. Mike couldn't cope with his guilt. He couldn't cope with life. His life was in turmoil. He probably felt like there was no one left who understood him after Anna died."

"He said that. He told me that Anna was the only person who loved him. But, it wasn't true. I loved him. I never told him that as much as I probably should have." Charles' body shook with sobs.

Chapter Twenty-Nine

The afternoon of Mike's funeral, Jessie, John, Amanda, and the rest of his friends stood outside the small funeral home waiting their turn inside. Quiet and subdued, they stood in a small tight circle holding hands.

"Jessie, when did you talk to Mike last?" John asked.

"I don't know. Couple weeks ago, I guess. He never called me back when I'd leave messages."

"How horrible for his dad." Amanda sniffled into a tissue. "I heard my parents talking last night. They said that Mike committed suicide because he killed Anna."

"No way, Mike loved her." John said.

"They did fight a lot." Jessie said.

"I guess we'll never know the whole story." John replied. "Hey, they're letting everyone in, let's go."

❧❧

Katherine sat in the row behind Charles Beckett. Earlier, she'd been briefly introduced to Mike's mother, Megan. The encounter had been awkward, especially knowing the circumstances surrounding the divorce. Katherine had murmured her condolences then hurried away feigning an excuse to speak to someone else.

She bowed her head during the service and tried not to compare this one to her daughter's or even to her husband's.

Instead of focusing on the tragedy of death, Katherine sought to concentrate on the positive influence the new teen center would have on the community. And, most of all, she prayed that this would be the end of senseless, needless death in their community.

❧❧

Jessie nudged John in the ribs. "Hey, who's that lady with Mike's dad?"

"I dunno, maybe it's Mike's mom."

"Did you ever hear Mike talk about his mom?"

"Nope. Never." John leaned over and whispered to Amanda, "Did you ever know Mike to talk about his mom?"

"I thought she was dead." Amanda whispered back.

"Amanda said she thought Mike's mom was dead."

"Dead? He never said that to me."

John leaned back to whisper to Amanda, "Jessie says he never said anything about his mom being dead to her."

"Well, tell the little twerp that Mike didn't always tell her everything."

"I will not." John shushed her then said, "Behave yourself."

Jessie poked John, "Hey, look, there's Mrs. Marshall, Anna's mom!" she said in an excited whisper.

"Yeah, so, ouch, that hurts."

"Look, she's leaning over to say something to Mike's dad."

John pushed Jessie back down into her seat. "Sit still, behave yourself, you're at a funeral for God's sake."

Jessie tried to see over the heads in front of her. "Wouldn't that be so cool if those two got together?"

Amanda leaned over John, "Jessie, you're such a child."

Jessie proved her right by sticking her tongue out at her.

✐∾

Janis poked her head into Helen McDougal's office. "Chief, there's a phone call for you."

Helen looked up from the pile of paperwork strewn across her desk. "Thanks, Janis. Any idea who it is?"

"Assistant D.A. Louden. Says he's looking for the report on the Beckett kid."

Helen pushed papers around on her desk. "Where did I put that report?"

"It's right here, Chief. I put it aside because I thought you might be looking for it."

"Thanks, Janis, you've really been a big help lately. Remind me to talk to you later, okay?"

Janis nodded as she left the Chief Medical Examiner's office. She hoped that Helen wanted to talk to her about the promotion's list that was to be posted next week.

Helen picked up the telephone, "Hello, Sam."

"Hi, Helen. I guess you know why I'm calling."

"Yes, I do. I have the report right here. These are the hardest cases, you know. The kids. Hey, weren't you trying to prosecute this kid for the death of his girlfriend a few months ago?"

"Unfortunately, yes. Come to find out, he left a note claiming he really did kill her."

"Oh, God, Sam, how awful. How are his parents handling it?"

"Probably just like any other parent who found their son had put a gun to his head and pulled the trigger."

"It was a clean wound. He died instantly. I know that's not much comfort to the family, but it's the best I can do. Other than that, we found nothing in his stomach. It looked like he hadn't eaten in days. His blood alcohol level was 0.012 and he tested positive for GHB and cannabis."

"Thanks, Helen. Looks like we'll close the books on these two cases. There isn't much left to go on. I think the families of both these kids have been through enough."

⁂

"Mags, it's been a nightmare these last few days."

"I can only imagine, hon. How you holding up?"

"Actually, much better than I thought I would. I'm amazed I've made it this far."

"You said that Anna's boyfriend killed her then he couldn't remember, then he did, then he killed himself over it?"

"Well, that's basically what happened. Apparently, Mike, that was Anna's boyfriend, proposed to her that night and she said no. I guess with the combination of drugs and alcohol he lost his temper and hurt her. He hurt her too much. He drowned her. I guess the combination of the drugs and his guilt blocked it from his memory for awhile."

"Is that possible?"

"This GHB, or Ecstasy, or whatever they're calling it now, has some affect on short term memory. Studies are still being done. But, the problem was that when Mike remembered he was so overwrought with guilt that he couldn't live with himself."

"How horrible for his family."

"Do you remember who Mike's father was?"

"Wasn't he the reporter that's been giving you such a hard time?"

"You got it. He came here the night Mike died. He wanted to tell me first before I heard it on the news or read it in the paper."

"I hope you gave him the old what for!"

"Actually, I was furious. But it was only at first. Then, I worked through my anger and realized I had to get past it. He needed help. That man was truly remorseful."

"Katie, you sound like you're doing much better. How is your crusade going for the teen center?"

"That's the other thing I wanted to talk to you about. Charles Beckett plans on making his support public. This situation with his son has helped him see that our community needs to address the drug and alcohol problems among the teenagers."

"How wonderful!"

"Sort of."

"Right, I know. It's horrible that his son had to die before he could see."

"Well, we're not going to let our children's deaths be for nothing."

"I'm proud of you, Katherine. I know you're going to succeed."

"Thanks. Oh, I talked to mother yesterday. She says that the doctors are trying a new treatment. What do you know about this?"

"I talked to the doctor and he said the prognosis is good. That's all we can hope for now."

"I understand. I just wish ..."

"Don't go borrowing trouble, Katie. Just be grateful you still have some time together. I gotta tell you, mamma doesn't hold a grudge. She understands."

"I am grateful. I am."

"I watched the weather earlier. Looks like you have another tropical storm heading your way."

"Don't worry. Its predicted path is hundreds of miles south of us. If it ever comes this way at all. The forecasters are predicting it will turn west before it reaches the Keys."

"Do you have enough flashlights? Batteries? Candles? Fresh water?"

Katherine laughed into the phone. "Yes, yes, yes, and yes. I stay stocked and renew my hurricane kit every year. We'll probably only get some rain, which we can use anyway."

"All right. I'll take your word for it. You live there and know what you're doing. I hope your meeting with the city council goes well, Katie. Give them hell."

"Thanks, Mags. Kiss Hank and hug the grandkids for me."

"Will do."

Chapter Thirty

"You want to what?"

"You heard me, Joe."

"You want to write an official apology to Katherine Marshall in your next column."

Charles nodded.

"Are you friggin' nuts?" Joe flung his arms out, nearly knocking over papers stacked on the desk. "Oh, hey, I know you just lost your kid, but take some time off. Give you a chance to get your head back together."

"My head is fine. And, I didn't 'lose' my kid. It's not like I can *find* him again." Charles gave Joe a look of disgust. "Besides, I've already taken enough time off. I need to get back to work. I'm losing my mind without anything to do."

Joe had the graciousness to look embarrassed. "Well, you know what I meant."

"Yeah, right." He turned in his chair away from his editor. "I'm going to do this."

"Hey, it's your career that's going down the tubes."

"I don't think so, not this time."

※ ※

Nick parked his truck in the same spot he used every school year. He enjoyed getting to school early, before the students. It gave him some quiet time to prepare his lessons as well as just a chance to take a deep breath before the day started.

Grabbing his thermos and newspaper he made his way into the teacher's lounge through the short hallway that would soon be filled with children.

He poured himself a cup of special blend coffee that he ground and blended from beans he chose himself. He sipped it while he read the paper.

"Holy Shit!" he exclaimed.

"What?" another teacher walked into the lounge just as Nick made his exclamation.

"Do you remember at the end of last school year, start of the summer, that girl died from drowning?"

"Yeah, I think so, wasn't there some sort of hearing or trial?"

"Right. They charged the boyfriend for giving her drugs that caused her to drown. But it didn't stick. He was acquitted."

"Yeah, I remember. His dad was some reporter for the newspaper and he made a big deal about single parents and stuff. It caused some major arguments in our family. My sister is raising her kids on her own and she had a few choice words to say every time another column came out."

"Take a look at this." Nick passed the paper over to the other teacher.

"Holy Shit!"

"Yeah, my sentiments exactly."

"Today isn't April first, right? This really says what I think it says?"

"Looks that way. The great Charles Beckett making a public apology. I never thought I'd see the day."

"You mind if I cut this out?"

"Yeah, as a matter of fact I do. I want to send it to a friend."

"Okay, I gotta run. I'm gonna go get a paper and cut the article out for my sister. I'll be back before the first bell."

"You better be. Your class is a handful. I wouldn't want to be the one who has to cover for you."

⚜

"Katherine, have you seen the paper today?"

"Good morning to you too, Jennie. And, yes, I have seen the paper." Katherine swung her briefcase onto the chair in front of her desk. She pulled out her own copy and waved it in her secretary's face.

"I'm sorry, good morning. I was so excited when I read the paper this morning that I couldn't wait to show it to you. Of course, I should have realized you'd have your own copy."

"It's okay, I don't blame you for being excited. Charles Beckett wrote an awesome article. The death of his son made a huge impact on his life. His support for the teen center means a lot to our cause."

⚜

Charles stared at the phone in his hand. He'd just dialed Katherine Marshall's number without realizing it. Should he hang up? Does she have caller ID? He had this overwhelming urge to talk to her and he didn't understand why.

"Hello?"

"Oh, hi, I'm sorry, did I catch you at a bad time?"

"Charles?"

"Yeah, I'm sorry. I really don't know why I called. I guess I just needed to talk to someone who might understand ... uh ... me and what I'm going through."

"I do. And, you can call me anytime. What can I do for you?"

"I guess you've read the paper by now?"

"Yes, I did, and I think you did a great job. Your apology wasn't the least bit pathetic."

"Pathetic? Interesting you chose that word."

"I think you were very brave to write what you did."

"Well, I have to tell you that we're getting a lot of mixed messages from the public. Right now we're running about 60/40 when it comes to doing something about the teenagers."

"That's good, right?"

"Right."

"Uh, Charles, would you like to come to dinner tonight? Nothing special, just barbeque some grouper on the grill and a salad?"

"Oh, well, that's awfully nice of you, uh ... Katherine. I wasn't calling to wrangle a dinner invitation."

"I know. You want someone to talk to. Who says that we can't talk over dinner?"

"You're right. Shall I bring the wine?"

"Not for me, but you can bring a bottle for yourself."

"No, I really don't want alcohol, especially after this whole issue with Mike. Tell you what, I'll bring some of that sparkling water, how's that sound?"

"It sounds great. About 7 o'clock?"

"Perfect, I'll see you then."

⌇⌇

Katherine pulled herself together after the confusing call from Charles Beckett. Why did she invite him to dinner? She pretended that she was going to use her therapist skills to help him through this difficult time. *Are you sure that's all it is?*

I want to get his support, that's all. She scolded herself.

Katherine pulled herself out of her woolgathering and concentrated on her next project. She reviewed her plan for a new support group.

"Jennie," she called out to her assistant, "did you get the copy for the new ad?"

Jennie appeared in the doorway with a manila folder. "Sure did, it looks great. Very tasteful."

"Thanks." Katherine felt proud of her latest endeavor. After having just experienced a death in her family, and now watching Charles Beckett handle his situation, she realized that what the community needed was a special support group. A network of volunteers that would be there for those who needed them and would give parents or other family members support. The volunteers could listen with compassion and understanding about a death in their family. Only someone who had actually gone through the motions could truly understand how someone else would feel. She hoped to build a support network of men, women, and children who could relate to others in their time of need.

Jennie rushed into Katherine's office. "Katherine, your next appointment is here, but before I send him in, you've got to read this letter."

Katherine took the letter from Jennie's outstretched hand. The short three paragraphs were on quality letterhead. She scanned the letter quickly, then re-read it.

"I can't believe this!" Katherine smiled at Jennie who was beaming.

"I know. I know. I mean, I was sure you'd get it, but just seeing it in writing puts it all in perspective, you know?"

Katherine laughed at Jennie's excited chatter. "This means lots of work."

"Who cares how much work it means. We can handle it!"

"I like your spirit." Katherine folded the letter and put it on the corner of her desk. "We'll talk about this after my next appointment."

"Katherine, I'm so proud of you."

"Thanks, Jennie, but getting this assignment would never have been possible without your support."

"You are going to make a difference. I just know it." Jennie gave her the thumbs up sign as she walked back to the reception area to show Katherine's next appointment in to her office.

While she had a few seconds to herself, Katherine twirled in her chair. What a major coup! Getting approval from the school board to go ahead with her counseling program at the high school made her day. Having the school's approval would make for a strong argument against the city council. Elation flushed through her. She was still beaming when her next appointment walked through her office door.

Chapter Thirty-One

"I have to say, that's the best grilled grouper I've had in a long time." Charles leaned back in his chair and patted his stomach.

"Thank you. I learned a few tricks when I was down in the Keys last year. Anna and I ..." her words trailed off as she remembered the relaxing week in Islamorada. She stood and picked up their plates and silverware.

"Let me clear; you cooked."

"Why don't we both clear. You rinse and I'll load the dishwasher."

"Deal." Charles piled plates and carried them to the sink. While he rinsed he watched from the corner of his eye while Katherine busied herself by preparing the dishwasher with soap and rinse liquid. He noticed the sad look in her eyes. Offhandedly, he said, "Can I ask you something?"

"Sure."

"When do we stop waking up in the morning expecting to see them?"

Katherine's hand stopped pouring the dishwasher soap. She took a deep breath. "Probably never."

"Yeah, I guess."

"But, that doesn't mean we'll always be sad. Eventually, we'll be able to think about them and be happy with our memories. But, we'll never stop missing them."

Charles rinsed the last of the dishes and handed them to Katherine. "The nights at home are the hardest."

"I know what you mean. I have my work to keep me busy during the day, but when evening comes, it gets more difficult."

"I still can't go into his room."

"It took me several weeks and several tries before I managed to get into Anna's room." Katherine finished wiping table and counter. "But, then, Anna didn't ... well, you know."

"I know. She didn't kill herself. My son killed her." Charles turned away and walked to the sliding glass doors. He stared out into the night.

Katherine let him have his moment of silence while she made

coffee. Once it started perking she returned to his side and touched his shoulder. "Charles?"

No response.

"I have something I want to show you."

He wiped his face, and then turned to the woman who spoke softly at his side. "What?"

"Take a seat in the living room, I'll be right there."

Charles gave her a puzzled look but obediently headed for the living room.

A few minutes later, Katherine sat next to him and placed a box on her lap. She opened it and pulled out the first item.

"Here, look at this."

Charles took the photograph from Katherine. "It's Mike."

"I thought you might want it. Anna had tons of photos in her room. I've sorted through them. There were a few here that I thought you might like to have."

He held the picture in his hands. Carefully, he touched his son's smiling face. "He didn't smile much around the house."

"If it's any consolation, I think teenagers are sullen by nature."

"They are, aren't they?"

"It's their defense mechanism against the world."

"I suppose."

"Charles, I ... found going through the pictures therapeutic. Anna loved taking pictures. She documented much of her life with pictures and in words in her journals."

"Journals?"

"Anna kept diaries, journals if you will. She put most of her innermost thoughts on paper. At first, I was angry and hurt by what I read. The more I thought about it, and the more I learned about myself, I'm thankful that she left a part of her behind."

Charles nodded while he looked through the pictures.

"All I have left of Mike's words is his note." Charles tossed the pictures back in the box and leaned back against the sofa pillows.

"I know you're hurt right now. You have every right. But, that hurt will pass. Try and focus on the Mike you knew before the alcohol and before the drugs. Make those memories be the ones that you turn to when you want to remember your son."

"It's hard. All I can think about is him on his bed, and ... the blood... all that blood."

"Here, take these pictures. They'll help you put those other images out of your mind."

"Can I take a few of these pictures with Anna too?"

"Please, I'd like that. I know you probably didn't get a chance to know Anna very well. Maybe these will help. Here's something else that might help." Katherine handed Charles a few notebooks.

"What are these?"

"Anna's journals."

"Are you sure you want me to read these?"

"Yes, I am. I struggled with myself for the last few days about whether or not I wanted you to read them. Especially, after those horrible columns you wrote. But, I think you should know that I wasn't the perfect mother, Anna wasn't the perfect daughter, but together we were a family."

"I won't forget this, Katherine. This means a lot to me. Your generosity in sharing your daughter with me, and your forgiveness for my actions, and my son's ..." He turned his face away and pretended to study the fireplace.

"Hey, it's partially selfish on my part too, you know?"

"How's that?"

"I'm hoping that you'll help me convince the last of the nay-sayers that a teen center is just what this community needs."

"I'll do what I can."

"Thanks, that's all I ask." Katherine smiled for a second then a serious look passed over her face. "I have to tell you, there is some pretty graphic stuff in Anna's journal. Some of it might be hard for you to understand. Mike and Anna had an abusive relationship. I didn't know." Katherine shook her head.

"What?"

"It's difficult to fathom. I only have Anna's words. She never told me. She didn't tell me a lot of things."

"What do you mean?"

"Just be prepared. She and Mike, were, well ... they were intimate."

"I figured as much. I tried to talk to him about responsibility and birth control, as well as protection from sexually transmitted diseases."

"Same here, but it's difficult. They seem to know so much more than we do."

"I know, the same old machismos attitude from every teenager. They act like they know it all, but when it comes right down to it, they're blinded by not wanting to be the only one asking questions."

"I'm telling you this because there was an episode earlier in the school year that I only learned about by reading the journals."

"Oh?"

"Apparently Anna was pregnant."

"What?" Charles nearly dropped the box of pictures.

"It's almost surreal, if you think about it. We both were so close to being grandparents and we never knew. Now, we'll never have the ..." Katherine stood. "We need coffee. I'm sure it's ready by now."

"Coffee ... yeah, that's what we need." Charles licked his lips. He knew his body craved a drink, but he refused to give in. He called out to Katherine, "I hope it's strong."

By the time the pot of coffee was empty, Katherine and Charles discovered an inexplicable comfort in a shared suffering that brought them closer together in a mutual quest to prevent others from going through the same trauma.

They promised each other that they wouldn't let this tragedy ruin their lives. They vowed to stay positive and turn their energy into constructive action. They formulated a plan to reach out to the community by using national resources to bring focus on the issues and identify preventative programs.

Katherine made a list of agencies to contact. The National Mental Health Association, Suicide Prevention Advocacy Network, U.S. Surgeon General, The Louis de la Parte Mental Health Institute at the University of South Florida, National Institute on Drug Abuse, and the Center for Disease Control and Prevention topped the list.

Charles offered to split the list with her and ask his contacts at the newspaper for assistance.

Chapter Thirty-Two

Charles' newspaper articles returned, but with a renewed purpose—to take up Katherine's cause. The support was overwhelming. He never felt so good about his purpose in life. It gave him improved confidence.

Only one person wasn't happy about the change in Charles. His editor called him into his office.

"What in the hell is this shit you've been submitting?"

"I don't have time for this. I'm on my way to a press conference. I'll talk to you when I get back."

"No, you'll talk to me about it now."

"Look Joe, you know me. When I'm right I'll go the whole nine yards, but when I'm wrong, I'm the first to admit it."

"I think we've beaten this subject to death. Give it a rest. It's time for you to get back to your old self. I want to see controversy. Next column, got it?"

Charles looked sideways at his editor. "Why? I thought I had free reign to cover whatever issue I wanted to?"

"You did, but that was before you lost your edge." Joe threw his pen across the room in disgust. "You're no good to me now."

"Is that so? Then, maybe we should talk about my contract when I get back."

Checking his watch, Charles rushed into his office and threw a notebook, tape recorder, research material, and a list of questions into his briefcase.

The cameraman assigned to Charles poked his head through the doorway. "Yo, man, let's go."

"On my way, just give me a sec."

Realizing he had put Anna's journals into his briefcase to return to Katherine on his way home from work, he pulled them out to make room for his notes.

"Tick tock, tick tock." The cameraman tapped his watch.

"Shit, all right, I'm coming." Charles tossed the notebooks into a desk drawer, making a mental note to remind him where he put them and hurried out of his office to follow the trotting cameraman.

~~

"Hello, Mrs. Marshall."

"Yes?" Katherine answered the front door. The nicely dressed young man on the front step looked slightly uncomfortable. There was something about his eyes that gave her a sense of familiarity.

"It's me, Nick Mancuso. Your lawn service?" He realized she didn't recognize him.

"Oh, right. Nick. I'm sorry. I haven't seen you for a while. Someone else has been cutting the lawn." She regained her composure and asked him in. Katherine led the young man to the lanai behind her house and asked him to take a seat.

"Would you like some iced tea?"

"Sure, that'd be great."

Katherine retrieved the pitcher of sweet tea from the refrigerator and poured the cold amber liquid into two frosty glasses from the freezer.

"Here you go, nice and cold." Katherine handed the young man a frosty glass.

"Thanks." He drank to satisfy his thirst then went on, "I only work for the lawn service during the summer. I teach during the other part of the year."

"Really? I didn't know that." Katherine recalled the last time Nick was in her home. She felt remiss for not speaking to him since then.

Nick seemed to have read her mind. "Mrs. Marshall, Katherine if I may?"

Katherine nodded.

"Katherine, Ever since that day when you told me about your daughter, I haven't been able to put it out of my mind. It touched me in a way that has impacted my life."

"I'm flattered, I think." Katherine looked at the young man seated across from her.

"I teach at the private school across town. High school-level. Teenagers."

She nodded.

"We've been watching your success at the high school and we'd like to implement the same program at our school."

"That's great. I think that would be a wonderful idea."

"I know you are only one woman and you're probably being pulled in a dozen directions at once. Adding another school to your schedule wasn't probably high on your list. So, I'd like to offer my services."

"I don't think I quite understand." Katherine sat the iced tea glass on the low table in front of her and leaned forward.

"I want to work with you. I want you to teach me about your program and I'll take it back to my school." Nick reached out to touch Katherine on the hand and then leaned back. "I admire you very much.

You are truly an inspiration."

Katherine ducked her head and blushed. "Thank you. Thank you very much." If she didn't know better, she'd say that this handsome young man was flirting with her.

Nick put his nearly empty iced tea glass on the table next to his elbow then opened the paper bag he had carried into the house. In his hand he held a picture frame. "This is for you. I thought you might appreciate it." He handed it to Katherine.

Katherine took the frame from Nick and turned it over. A laugh escaped her lips.

"You don't like it?" He nearly pouted at the thought.

"Nick, I love it. It's perfect!" Katherine smoothed a hand over the front of the frame. Pressed between the glass and a muted mauve matting was the apology article by Charles Beckett. She reached a hand out and squeezed Nick's. "Thank you."

"I thought you might like it. I want to be your friend, Katherine."

"I'd like that."

"Good. Now, what do you say about celebrating our friendship by going out to dinner tonight?"

Katherine's jaw dropped open. He was asking her out! "Look, Nick, I really appreciate the offer, but ..."

Nick jumped in to fill the pause. "Hey, just friends, okay? We'll just take it slow. I really want to be a part of your program and help with the teen center. Anything else ..." he spread his hands. "We'll just take it as it comes, okay?"

Smiling, Katherine nodded. Inside, she was quaking. Was she ready for a relationship? Was she ready for a relationship with a man younger than herself?

~*~

"Hey, Beckett, you in here?" Joe called out as he walked into Charles Beckett's office.

Joe Splanto fumed at finding Beckett's office empty. He was furious at the direction Beckett was taking his columns. He needed controversy to sell papers. Harping on the needs of teenagers wasn't his idea of award winning journalism, unless it was filled with juicy morsels to keep the readers coming back for more.

Deciding to leave Beckett a note, he searched the desk for paper and pen. He pushed papers around in a desk drawer. Pulling out a notebook, he flipped through it for a blank sheet. "Oh shit, what do we have here?" Joe Splanto sat in Beckett's chair and turned to the first page of the notebook. He read quickly, devouring the revealing contents. "This is good." He murmured as he read. "Perfect, just perfect."

His mouth watered as he read. "Charlie, my boy, you are going to have one hell of a comeback article tomorrow!"

≈≈

Katherine swore she'd never go out on a work night again. Her evening with Nick had been fun and restful. It did her a world of good to go out and behave like a regular human being for a few hours. But, she was paying for it this morning. Late for work, Katherine had to make do with one cup of coffee and managed only a few sips between showering and getting dressed. On her way out the door, she stuffed the morning paper into her briefcase to read at the office.

Walking into the office, the telephone was ringing. She found Jennie asking someone to hold while she picked up the other line. Jennie waved frantically to catch her attention.

"What's going on?" Katherine asked.

"Have you read this morning's paper?"

"Not yet, didn't have time this morning." Katherine poured herself a cup of coffee from the pot Jennie already had made.

Jennie put another caller on hold then turned back to her boss. "Just read what that skunk, Beckett wrote in this morning's article." She punched another blinking button on the telephone.

Katherine carried her cup of coffee into her office and pulled out the newspaper. She turned to the local section and opened the paper to Beckett's column.

Coffee spewed from her mouth after reading the first line. She raced back to Jennie's desk and waved the paper in front of her. "Did you read this?"

"I know, I know. I want to put my hands around his neck and ..." Jennie made twisting motions with her hands.

"He has a lot of explaining to do." Katherine turned on her heel and headed back to her office. "Hold my calls until I get through to Beckett."

Furious, Katherine's hands shook as she punched Beckett's home number on the telephone. She seethed while the ring sounded in her ear. She left a scathing message on his answering machine then slammed the receiver down. She flipped through her address book to find the number to his office. That number also rang until his recorded message told her that he was either out of the office or on another line.

Unable to sit and wait for Beckett to call her back, Katherine grabbed her purse and rushed by Jennie as she headed for the door. "Jennie, I'm going to find that snake. I don't know how long it'll take. If you need me, call my cell phone."

"Sure thing, Katherine. I'll cover for you here."

Katherine pushed her way into the newspaper office and insisted that she speak to Charles Beckett immediately. The receptionist said she'd try his office, but he wasn't answering his calls.

"That's not good enough. Page him, please."

"Ma'am, we don't have a paging system here. I can ask someone to check and see if he's in yet."

"I'm not leaving until I speak to him." Katherine folded her arms across her chest.

The receptionist made another call to Beckett's desk. "I'm sorry, ma'am, I'm not getting any answer. I can take a message if you'd like."

Katherine kept a tight rein on her temper. She knew it wasn't this girl's fault for the article in this morning's paper. But, she knew whose fault it was and she was going to find him. "Thank you for trying. I'll find him myself." She rushed past the desk and found herself in a maze of cubicles. She hurried down the hall as the receptionist called for her to return.

Katherine scanned the faces in each cubicle, searching for one familiar face. The place was huge; it'd take hours to find someone in here without knowing where to look.

Swallowing the lump away in her throat, Katherine called out, "Charles Beckett!"

Heads turned. Katherine ignored the curious looks and asked the nearest group of people where she could find Beckett's office. She followed the pointing hands until she stood in front of a closed door. Katherine knocked and without waiting to be invited in she opened the door.

"Charles Beckett, you low-lying, scum-sucking snake. I'm going to ..." Katherine walked into Beckett's office.

Chapter Thirty-Three

"You son of a bitch, what in the hell were you thinking?"

"Back off, Beckett." Joe backed up as Beckett threatened him from across the desk.

"No way. Of all the low down, slime-ball cheap tricks you could have done, this is the worst."

"News is news. It's our job to report it. You seemed to have forgotten that."

"This isn't some two-bit, supermarket gossip rag, we don't print shit like that." Beckett slammed his hand on the desk. "You seemed to have forgotten that!"

"Look, Beckett, okay, I probably shouldn't have put your name on it, but other than that, what was the real harm?"

"You hurt a lot of innocent people, Splanto. Katherine Marshall for one. The memory of her daughter for another. All the people who had faith in her as a therapist for another."

"What's so different about what I wrote than what you were writing earlier?" Splanto reached for the telephone.

"Don't even think about it." Beckett knocked the phone off the desk. "Don't compare the trash you wrote to anything I've ever written." Beckett made his way around the desk and grabbed his editor by the throat. He pushed him until he lay across the desk. "You went too far this time, Splanto. Too far and you're going to pay for it."

"Help! Somebody help me, he's gonna kill me!"

"You wish," Beckett pulled his fist back, "you'll just wish you were dead."

"Beckett!"

Charles Beckett turned to see Katherine standing in the doorway. "Just in time to witness justice, Mrs. Marshall."

"Beckett, you ... you ..." Now that Katherine was face to face with the object of her anger she lost the words.

"You're a witness, lady. This guy is trying to kill me."

"Oh, shut up, Splanto." Beckett turned to Katherine. "Look, I can explain ..."

"Explain? I'd love to hear it. I'd love to hear how you took my daughter's precious words, and threw them into my face. I'd love to hear how you betrayed my trust. Tell me that I didn't give you those journals in confidence. How you just couldn't resist a story and plastered it all over the papers for everyone to read." Angry tears covered Katherine's face. "Explain to me that, huh?"

"Look, I didn't—" Charles began.

"You didn't what?" Katherine interrupted. "You didn't think I'd mind? Hah! You slime-sucking lowlife! This time you've gone too far."

Charles let go of his editor's shirt and crossed the room to stand in front of Katherine Marshall. "Katherine—"

"Don't 'Katherine' me, you jerk." She slapped him hard across his face then pulled her arm back to slap him again.

His cheek reddened from the impact of her open palm. He tried again. "I didn't write the article."

Katherine's hand stopped in mid-air. "Of course you did, your name is on it."

Charles Beckett turned to the man who was sitting at the desk massaging his throat. "That son-of-a-bitch wrote it."

"But, how did he know ..."

"He found the notebooks in my desk. He thought my column needed some spicing up, so he concocted the whole thing."

Katherine dragged her purse behind her as she walked over to the desk. She stared down at the man sitting in the chair. "Why would you do such a thing?" Katherine sank into a chair across from the desk. "Why?"

The man sitting at the desk waved his hand in the air toward Charles. "He left me no choice."

"Right. That's what you think." Charles approached him with a menacing look on his face. "You think you had no choice before? You just wait until you hear what I have to say now. You are going to apologize to Mrs. Marshall, then you're going to print a retraction claiming full responsibility. Then you're going to turn in your resignation. You got that, Splanto?"

"And, if I don't?" Splanto tried to show some bravado.

Beckett leaned over the desk into his editor's face, "I'll go straight to the top and you'll face criminal charges for impersonation and libel. Then," he turned to Katherine, "I'm sure Mrs. Marshall would be happy to file suit against the paper and you personally for damages." Beckett made eye contact with Katherine, but spoke to Splanto, "If you resign now and write your retraction, you can leave here and find another place to peddle your garbage. If you don't, no respectable newspaper will ever hire you again. You'd be lucky to find work writing ad copy for a sleazy dirt rag."

Charles turned to the crowd that had gathered at the door. "And we have plenty of witnesses."

Katherine eyed the man behind the desk. "I'd be happy to sue you for damages."

Splanto looked from Mrs. Marshall to Charles Beckett then over to the doorway. He signed in resignation. "All right. You got it. I'll print the retraction tomorrow and turn in my resignation."

The crowd cheered.

Charles Beckett sat in the chair next to Katherine. "Start writing."

"And, don't forget to include how you support a new teen center for the city." Katherine said.

Chapter Thirty-Four

"I'd like to thank the mayor and the city council for having the foresight to believe in our dream." Katherine Marshall stood behind the wooden podium with tears shining in her eyes.

"A child is a gift—a gift that is given to us to guide and teach; but not a gift that we can keep to ourselves. We must pass that gift on to the world. We must have faith in that gift to go out into the world and be strong. It's our cumulative responsibility to make sure we provide our children with the right tools. Information is the number one tool we can provide. By building this teen center and staffing it with caring and concerned members of the community, we'll be showing our children by example how to succeed."

Katherine moved to one side of the podium as the mayor stepped up and stood by her side.

"I'd like to be the first to congratulate you, Mrs. Marshall for your commitment to our children. And, to show our appreciation, we'd like you to cut the ribbon and officially open the doors on Bridgeway's new Anna Marshall and Michael Beckett Teen Center!"

Katherine looked behind her. She motioned for Charles Beckett to stand with her. He trotted to her side and supported her arms while she used both hands to hold the giant-sized scissors. They snipped at the bright yellow ribbon and it fell into two pieces.

"We did it!" Charles shouted.

Katherine hugged the man who helped her make her dream come true. She whispered in his ear, "Thank you."

Epilogue

"Hey, John," Jessie called from across the room of the teen center as she maneuvered her way through a gauntlet of chairs, tables, and admiring pleas for her attention. The room was filled with teenagers. Jessie spent most of her spare time away from school as a volunteer and a member of the Teen Agency Council.

Her baggy parachute-like material pants made swishing noises with each step she took as the bottoms of the pants dragged along the tiled floor.

John looked up in time to see her break free of one hug and step into another. He hung his head and shook it slowly back and forth as she dropped into the chair next to him.

Jessie tossled his light brown hair with her green and white striped tipped nails.

"Wha-a-a-t?" she drawled with a teasing grin. "You know you're my favorite, John-John." She placed an arm around his shoulders and gave him a quick, firm peck on his cheek. "See?" She smiled and pointed at the bright orange imprint of her lips she left on his cheek. "I branded you. You're mine."

John knew she was only kidding but it felt good to hear her say the words anyway. He was going to miss her. He was going away to boot camp next week. He'd joined the Marine Corps after the recruiter gave a presentation at the teen center last week.

He felt good about his decision. He had a career path and a firm belief that he was finally going to belong somewhere.

Jessie tugged on his arm and pulled him to a clear space on the floor. "Dance with me soldier boy."

The End

About the Author

Vicki M. Taylor writes dramatic stories with strong women as her main characters.

A prolific writer of both novel length and short stories, she brings her characters to life in the real world. Her memberships include the National Association of Women Writers, Short Fiction Mystery Society, and many more. She has had hundreds of articles published in electronic and print publications.

She is one of the founders and past President of the Florida Writers Association, Inc. She conducts regular writing workshops, speaks to local writing groups, and facilitates a Reading Women's Fiction Group at her local Barnes and Noble bookstore.

When she's not writing, you can find her lurking about the many writing boards dispensing little pearls of wisdom from her computer in Tampa, Florida where she lives with her husband.

Want to know more about Vicki M. Taylor?

Vicki M. Taylor's official website is at vickimtaylor.com.

Printed in the United States
27790LVS00001B/229

9 781594 260513